VINNIE'S WAR

Also by David McRobbie
and published by Allen & Unwin

A Whole Lot of Wayne
Eugénie Sandler PI

VINNIE'S WAR

David McRobbie

ALLEN&UNWIN

First published in 2011

Allen & Unwin
83 Alexander Street
Crows Nest NSW 2065
Australia
Phone: (61 2) 8425 0100
Fax: (61 2) 9906 2218
Email: info@allenandunwin.com
Web: www.allenandunwin.com

A Cataloguing-in-Publication entry is available
from the National Library of Australia
www.trove.nla.gov.au

ISBN 978 1 74237 576 2

Teachers' notes available from www.allenandunwin.com

Cover and text design by Sandra Nobes
Front cover images: clouds/figures by Bradley Mason/iStockphoto;
   St Paul's Cathedral by Herbert Mason, 29-Dec-40
Back cover image from Britain at War by J.B. Priestley,
   Angus and Robertson Ltd, 1943
The images used for chapter openings are from WWII memorabilia
Photo on p190 is of Newton Academy class, Ayr, 1944 or 1945,
   by I. & S. Sternstein, Glasgow
Set in 11.5 pt Classic Garamond by Sandra Nobes
This book was printed in April 2011 at McPherson's Printing Group,
76 Nelson St, Maryborough, Victoria 3465, Australia.
www.mcphersonsprinting.com.au

10 9 8 7 6 5 4 3 2 1

For my grandchildren

EVACUATION
WHY AND HOW?

PUBLIC INFORMATION
LEAFLET   NO. 3

Read   this   and
keep   it carefully.
You may need it.

Issued from the Lord Privy Seal's Office July, 1939

Prologue
EUSTON STATION, LONDON
September 1940

Vinnie didn't want to be in this place, not with hundreds of miserable kids crowding around him. Everywhere he looked they were sobbing and carrying on as if their hearts would break. Their mums, too, were upset, and who could blame them? It wasn't every day a mother had to say goodbye to her children, then send them away on a train to wherever.

First chance Vinnie got, he planned to be off out of this chaos, back to the East End, bombs or no bombs. That's where he belonged and where he'd try his luck, but getting away wasn't going to be easy. A bothered-looking official from the town hall had escorted Vinnie and a bunch of other kids to the station that September morning. They'd all been rounded up for evacuation after being bombed out of their houses. *Thank you, Mr Hitler*, Vinnie thought, *bet you enjoyed your first air raid on London. We'll do the same for you some day – with knobs on.*

Vinnie felt raw and tearful at having to leave the pub where he'd lived and worked. Everything had happened so fast he hadn't even said a proper goodbye to the three most important people in his life. Instead, here he was, lined up in Euston Station, wearing a cardboard luggage label. It was tied on with string done up in a bow, and it told everyone that he was: 'VINCENT CARTWRIGHT. 13.' When the town hall man wasn't looking, Vinnie tugged the label off and crushed it under his shoe. If he couldn't be free, at least he could do that.

A distracted woman crouched nearby to comfort her small son. 'Oh, please don't make a fuss, Joey,' she whispered.

'You come with us, Mum,' Joey pleaded. 'You come on the train, too. Please.'

'No, I have work to do in London, Joey. But Kathleen will be with you, won't you, Kathleen?'

Joey's older sister took his hand. 'Of course I will, Joey. It'll be an adventure, you and me going off together.'

'But where are we going?'

'That's part of the adventure,' Kathleen encouraged her brother. 'It's a mystery. We'll find out when we get there.'

Kathleen, Joey and their mum were soon lost in the crowd. Then the town hall man, too overwhelmed to be polite, consulted a paper and called loudly to Vinnie's group, 'Right, boys and girls, pay attention here. Your train leaves from Platform Four.' He pointed. 'That way.'

There was a heavy iron gate at Platform Four, opened only just wide enough to let the evacuee kids through in single file. Once past that gate and on to a train, Vinnie would be trapped.

With no alternative, he sighed and followed the others.

FORM EV 2.

VISITOR'S RECORD FORM

819.

District ATCHAM

Ward or Parish

Berrington

Address 68. Cantlop.

Name of householder John H. Warren

Number of habitable rooms 5

4. N

Number for whom accom available within

Is the thinking condition for

Is the house charge of u

Is the househ bedding for th accommodated number of mat

*Any other comm   urly refus

the idea of hav

could obtain

for refuse

ote here
    e.g., old age or inf.
nied children; full part.

lingness to take others if unable to take unaccom-
other persons expected under private arrangements.

C
For use by Local Authority.

PROVISIONAL DECISION

of unaccompanied children

NUMBERS ACTUALLY TAKEN
(For use only if evacuation is carried out)

No. of unaccompanied
    children at 10/6

Chapter One

ONE YEAR EARLIER: LONDON, 1939

One summer morning as Vinnie Cartwright walked to school, he saw an unusual sight. The small and portly landlord of the corner pub was sweeping the pavement outside his front door – and not doing it very well. Vinnie pointed to a tram ticket at his foot and grinned, then called, 'Mr Rosen, you missed this bit.'

'Enough of your cheek, young Cartwright.' The landlord leaned on his broom, puffing slightly.

'Why are *you* sweeping up?' Vinnie persisted. 'Where's Aaron?'

'He's gone to join the Royal Air Force. Bloody war.'

'It might not start,' Vinnie said. 'Where there's hope...'

'It'll start. You'll see.'

'*I* could do Aaron's work,' Vinnie offered. 'Some of it, anyway. Before and after school. All day Saturdays, if you like.'

The landlord looked Vinnie up and down, then asked, 'How old are you, son?'

'Twelve – and I'm strong.'

'All right, Vinnie. I'll give you a go. See you at four, eh?'

'I'll be here, Mr Rosen. And don't forget that tram ticket.'

✳ ✳ ✳

The same afternoon, Vinnie collected four empty beer glasses from the top of the pub piano, then carried them behind the bar. Mrs Rosen, the landlord's wife, was washing up. 'Must say you're a brave one, Vinnie Cartwright. Brave as a lion.'

'Why's that?' he asked.

'Your Aunty Vera's not going to be happy with you working in a pub.'

'She doesn't need to know, does she?'

'Oh, Vinnie, Vinnie.' Mrs Rosen raised her eyebrows, shook her head, then made a song of it: '*If you knew Vera like I know Vera.*'

✳ ✳ ✳

There had been no father in Vinnie's life. Not one that he could remember, at least, although from time to time men had stayed in his mother's house, sometimes for as long as a fortnight. They were usually sailors, often rough and with little to say for themselves. Vinnie had learned to make himself scarce, sometimes spending a wintry night wandering the streets before creeping indoors again to see what his welcome would be.

When he was eleven, Vinnie's mother had died of the twin Ds – drink and depression, with a bit of poverty thrown in too. He was not on his own for long. Soon after a cheap funeral, a tall woman with a fox fur around her neck had said, 'Vincent, you're to stay with me.'

The only other place for him was the orphanage, where everyone knew that kids ate thin porridge and broke big stones all day with a hammer. He'd thought the woman didn't look the porridge type, so he agreed to go. Not that he'd much say in it, really.

'You can call me Aunty Vera.' The woman had managed a thin smile. It was to be her first and only.

Vinnie soon discovered that 'Aunty' Vera wasn't his aunt at all, but a foster-mother, approved by the welfare people at the town hall. She liked things to be 'nice'. And Vinnie wasn't. 'Oh dear,' she'd said when she got him home to her sparkling house and examined what was in his cardboard suitcase. 'Oh dear, oh dear.'

Vinnie's clothes had been clean enough, but ragged. He had two cotton shirts, one pair of short trousers, a woollen pullover with no sleeves, and pyjamas, top and bottom. There wasn't much else in the suitcase. 'Mum was poorly, see,' he tried to explain, 'at the end. All the money went on medicine and the doctors.'

Aunty Vera just sighed 'Oh dear' again, then rummaged in a deep trunk and ordered in a no-nonsense voice, 'Off with what you're wearing, Vincent.'

'What? With you looking at me?'

'Why would I look at you?' Aunty Vera demanded. So Vinnie cautiously took off his clothes. With a pair of tongs from the fireplace, she picked up his old trousers, then opened the door of the Aga cooker and stuffed them inside. His pants burst into flames.

Next Aunty Vera gave Vinnie a pair of green velvet short trousers that were too long for him, and big around the middle. Worse still, they had a large, decorative button on each leg, at the side hem.

'Did these belong to some girl?'

'No they did not,' Aunty Vera snapped. 'They belonged to my son, Archibald.'

Vinnie looked unhappily at his new shimmering trousers. 'In the circus, was he?'

'Archibald is a cook in the Royal Navy. Fighting for his King and country. Or he will be, when the war starts.'

Next to come was a shirt with a tail so long it hung out the bottom of Vinnie's velvet trousers. Vinnie tucked it between his legs and said, 'This is a nightshirt.'

'It is not, so be thankful for it.' Aunty Vera picked up his old shirt and poked it into the flames along with his trousers, which were blazing merrily. Vinnie wondered how he could go to school wearing this outfit.

Aunty Vera produced a pile of other garments that had belonged to Archibald. 'There's still a lot of wear in these, Vincent. We can't have you turning up at Sunday school looking like a vagrant, can we?'

Vinnie thought, *Sunday school, eh? Monday-to-Friday school, fair enough. But Sunday school, no. Not even a maybe.*

That had been the beginning of a war between Vinnie and Aunty Vera. Whenever he could, he'd resisted her, starting at a street market where he'd swapped Archibald's extravagant trousers for more ordinary clothes. Vinnie only went once to Sunday school before finding better ways to spend his day off. And most weekday mornings he went to school early; afternoons he stayed late, making use of the library. Anything was better than returning to Aunty Vera's cold but spotless house, where the mat at the back door didn't say 'WELCOME', but 'WIPE YOUR FEET'.

A job in the pub was just what he wanted.

* * *

Vinnie settled in well with Mr and Mrs Rosen, making himself useful, earning smiles and a few bob. Three weeks went by like this; then the other boy arrived.

Mr Rosen picked him up in London and brought him back to the pub one quiet afternoon. 'This is Isaac,' he announced to Vinnie. 'A Jewish lad who's managed to get out of Germany.'

'Just in time, I'd say.' Mrs Rosen embraced the boy warmly, then took a second or two to compose herself. In a voice that was now a whisper she said, 'We've been worried you'd not make it out, Isaac, but you are very welcome in our house.'

'Thank you,' Isaac replied. He was tall and thin, about fifteen, Vinnie guessed, with stooped shoulders and long black hair. 'You are so kind. My parents will soon escape to Britain too, I hope. Then we'll be a family again. Safe here.'

'Until that day, Isaac, you just make yourself right at home.' Mrs Rosen touched the boy's shoulder gently and ruffled his dark hair.

'But please, I must work, to pay for this, for your kindness.'

'There's no need,' Mrs Rosen assured him.

'Well…' Mr Rosen said. 'With Aaron away, perhaps we could do with some help, dear.' He looked at Vinnie and gave a small, apologetic shrug.

Vinnie understood. It had been a good job while it lasted.

* * *

On that late August night the pub was busier than usual. The newspapers and the BBC wireless said that war was getting closer, and people seemed to cling together, looking for support and hope. One loud voice at the bar shouted, 'If it starts, it'll all be over by Christmas.'

Someone else answered, 'That's what they said about the last war.'

Vinnie worked until closing time, when customers stumbled into the street singing the song 'There'll always be an England'. With nothing to do, he made his way back to Aunty Vera's house.

Vinnie tried to tiptoe in, but she'd been waiting up for him, nursing a sharp question: 'And what time do you call this, young man?'

'I was at a friend's place,' he lied, 'playing Monopoly.'

Aunty Vera sniffed the air around him. 'Tobacco! Vincent, have you been smoking?'

'No,' Vinnie said. That bit was true. The pub air was always thick with pipe and cigarette smoke. The smell clung to everything; to clothes and hair.

Aunty Vera stepped closer and sniffed again, then recoiled. 'Beer!' She almost spat the word at him. 'Beer! Not in my house. You've given me nine months of trouble. So, back to the town hall in the morning. We'll see if the welfare people will find a place for you – in the orphanage!'

That word came like a sting. Vinnie thought, *Anything but the orphanage*. In the pub he'd found things he'd never had before. Laughter, for a start. She would take it away from him – that and his freedom.

Vinnie looked at Aunty Vera and said, 'You can see the welfare if you want, but me? I'm off now.'

And he left her place right then and there, using the front door and not the back.

* * *

There was a shed in the pub yard, used for storing empty beer crates. Sneaking inside was no problem. Working in the darkness, Vinnie laid four beer crates end-to-end to form a bed, then used his suitcase for a pillow, making himself as comfortable as he could. This late in summer, the night was warm enough so that he'd not freeze.

He lay in the darkness, hands behind his head, and thought about things. With Isaac living in the pub, there would be no job for him anymore. That was plain – Mr Rosen's look had said it all. And Aunty Vera would report him to the welfare. He could hear her now: *The boy's utterly wilful, a heathen and a boozer who smokes like a factory chimney.* So who knew what the welfare people would do when they caught him? Or where they'd send him.

Sleep wouldn't come, and it wasn't because the beer crates were hard. He'd slept in much harder places; a shop doorway even. His mind drifting now, Vinnie remembered one of his mum's sailor friends who'd come back on his ship from somewhere tropical. The man had said, 'Here y'are, son. Brought you a Christmas box. All the way from West Africa.' The gift was a parcel, wrapped in glittery paper and tied with a ribbon. Inside was a big, rough lump of raw, unprocessed chocolate. It didn't look like a chocolate bar that came out of the machine at the Underground station – this chocolate was so hard Vinnie had to break it with the coal hammer. When he finally managed to get a bit small enough to go in his mouth, it was so bitter he spat it straight out.

The man enjoyed his joke, and Vinnie had pretended to because his mum said he was a big boy now and had to learn to take a few ups and downs.

But was his life always to be like that; always to be the butt of somebody's unkind trick?

He mused in the darkness: *You find a good thing, enjoy it for a while, until it gets ripped away.*

Vinnie slept, and woke in the morning still bitter. He'd have to find a new place to live, and the earlier the better. Then someone began playing the piano. Vinnie recognised it as the old piano in the pub, for he'd heard it often enough, hammering out rumpy-tump, daisy-daisy sorts of tunes for a beery singsong.

But this sound was different. It was a melody he'd never heard before, and it touched him and soothed him like no music had ever done. Vinnie had to see who was playing. He got off his beer-crate bed and tiptoed to the pub. A street clock said the time was ten past five. The music was louder here, but no less beautiful.

Inside the pub, he found the Jewish boy, Isaac, seated at the piano with a faraway look in his eyes. He was off somewhere in a private world of the music he was making. In the background, still in their dressing gowns, stood Mr and Mrs Rosen, watching and listening. Mrs Rosen caught sight of Vinnie and put a finger to her lips, so he'd not interrupt. It was a warning Vinnie didn't need.

He could almost feel the music inside him. His spine tingled and the hair on the back of his neck rippled. No one spoke, or moved, as Isaac played on. Vinnie wished it would never stop.

How to keep well in Wartime

ISSUED FOR THE
MINISTRY OF HEALTH
BY THE MINISTRY
OF INFORMATION

Chapter Two
SCUM OF THE EARTH!

Isaac played on for a minute or two, crouched over the piano keys, then realised Vinnie was watching and listening intently. 'Ah, Vinnie. I disturb you.' He raised his fingers from the keyboard.

'No, don't stop. Don't stop playing, not for me. Please.'

'Nor for us, Isaac.' Mr Rosen came into the bar, clapping his hands as he approached. 'That was marvellous. Such a tune, to be wrung out of that old piano, eh?'

'To think we'd hear such fine sounds in this place.' Mrs Rosen beamed and nodded. 'Bravo, Isaac. Bravo!'

Isaac smiled shyly as he faced them. 'Thank you. My first audience in Britain.'

'May there be many more,' Mr Rosen said, then turned to Vinnie. 'And why are you here so early, young Vinnie?'

Mrs Rosen had already guessed the reason. 'I bet it was Aunty Vera.' She laughed. 'Come on, have some breakfast and tell us the sad story.' Mrs Rosen ushered Vinnie and Isaac into the pub kitchen, singing, '*If you knew Vera*,' in an amused sort of way.

* * *

It was settled over breakfast. Vinnie would keep working in the pub, but better still, he and Isaac could share the spare bedroom upstairs. When Aaron came home on leave from the RAF, they'd sort something out. To keep up his studies, Isaac would use the piano when the pub was shut. 'Perhaps I could play for the customers,' he suggested.

Mr Rosen frowned. 'M-mm, don't know about that, son. Folk from around here might not take to Beethoven and Schubert.'

'Then I'll play other things. They can ask me. I play anything. *If You Knew Susie*, I play that too.'

Vinnie remained worried. Mr Rosen noticed his glum look. 'Why the long face, Vinnie?'

'Aunty Vera's sending the welfare after me.'

Mrs Rosen brushed this aside. 'There's a war coming, Vinnie. The welfare's got enough to be thinking about. Besides, you have a home here. That's what we'll tell them.'

Vinnie cheered up and looked around the kitchen. It was good to belong.

* * *

Starting that very night, Isaac's mellow notes from the old upright piano floated out into the street. People were attracted to the pub because it was bright there, and cheerful. As time passed, Vinnie noticed more and more customers in military uniform; strange faces with different accents from all over Britain, every man and woman keen to share an hour or two in friendly company. Isaac's music made the pub a welcoming place.

Customers could join in the singing, or just listen to this young chap playing any tune they could name. Someone only had to whistle or hum a few bars and Isaac would feel out the notes, then play the song – just like that, with half a smile on his face, his fingers flying over the keys. At other times he played his own music, and the whole pub fell quiet. His audience might not be able to tell the name of these pieces, but they knew what the music was doing to them.

Mrs Rosen would whisper to her husband, 'The boy's too good for that piano. We should get him a better one.'

'Or get him on the BBC,' Mr Rosen would respond. 'He should be heard.'

Then came September the third of that year, 1939, and the war began. Two years earlier the world had seen what Adolf Hitler's bombs did in the Spanish city of Guernica. Fearing this, many parents sent their children away to the safety of the country. But Vinnie and Isaac decided to stay in London, and Mr and Mrs Rosen respected their choice.

＊　＊　＊

As the two of them lay each night in their beds in Aaron's old room upstairs Isaac was at first quiet, but late one night soon after the war had begun he started to speak about his life in Germany. 'I was studying music,' he began, 'but everywhere in the country the Nazis make life difficult for us Jews.'

'You mean, like bullying?' Vinnie asked.

'A stronger word is *Verfolgung*,' Isaac said. 'Persecution. We are not allowed to work, to run a business or attend school or university. We have to wear a yellow cloth badge saying *Jude*, which is *Jew*. As if we are infectious. A disease.'

'So you left home?'

'That was not an easy thing.' There was a long silence; then Isaac continued: 'To smuggle me out of the country, my father paid a huge bribe. Sold possessions for a small price. Then he and *Mutti* – that is my mother – they said farewell to me and promised to come later. But...' He sighed.

Vinnie knew that Isaac hadn't heard anything from Germany. They lay quietly for a while, each with their own thoughts. At last, desperate for something to say, Vinnie asked, 'Did you have a piano at home, Isaac?'

'Oh, yes, a large one. A grand piano. A Broadwood, it was. I expect some Nazi has it now, along with the other things my parents owned.'

'They take anything they fancy? Just like that?'

'It's what they do.'

'You've got nothing left, then?'

'Only some clothes, and this,' Isaac responded. Vinnie couldn't see anything in the darkness, but he heard the sad notes of a harmonica. Isaac played gently for a minute or two, then stopped and said, 'I'm tired now, Vinnie. So let's sleep, eh? And what shall we dream about?'

It was a game they'd invented – to tell each other their favourite dream. Isaac's was to have things the way they used to be: family, home, country and piano. Vinnie dreamed of having a place where he belonged forever. He had found a home in the pub, but like other things in his life, he feared it could be ripped away from him; another unkind trick. Over time, though, inspired by hearing Isaac play, Vinnie's dream had slowly changed. If he had music, then that would always be with him. He'd seen the effect as Isaac tried out a new tune: when he got it right, and the pub customers approved, Isaac's confidence grew; then he would smile. It was the only time he showed any joy. Isaac and music belonged together. One was made for the other.

Vinnie could belong, too. This night he said shyly, 'Isaac, my dream is to play the way you do.'

'The harmonica? I have two of them. You can have one, Vinnie.'

'Thanks, Isaac, but I really mean the piano. I want to play the piano.'

'Okay, I'll teach you,' Isaac offered, as if it was the simplest thing in the world. 'We start tomorrow. Now, let's dream.'

*　*　*

The next morning Isaac and Vinnie rose at five o'clock, because at other times the pub was busy. When Vinnie lifted the lid on the old piano, Isaac commented, 'That was the easy part. Now comes the hard work.'

The lesson was no more than finding where the notes were, and playing a simple scale. On that first morning, they went for an hour and Vinnie's wrists ached. He was disappointed not to ripple his fingers over the keys and make the music pour out, the way Isaac did. But after a week, Vinnie realised music was not going to come easily. Nor could he give up – especially since Isaac gained such pleasure and purpose from their lessons.

Winter approached and the mornings grew colder, so they wrapped blankets around themselves, then played the piano. At Christmas, the war news from Europe continued to be bad; it seemed there would be no stopping Hitler. Since London remained peaceful, parents who'd evacuated their children in September 1939 began bringing them home again. The city was safe, they thought.

Most young students of music had one lesson a week; Vinnie had a session every morning. Mr and Mrs Rosen approved so much of Isaac's daily teaching that they had the piano tuned. At times when the pub was quiet, Mrs Rosen would say, 'Vinnie, do your practice.'

He also picked out tunes on the harmonica Isaac had given him. Vinnie found he could play as he swung beer crates in the yard or did other tasks that only needed one hand.

* * *

In late August 1940, Vinnie gave his first public piano recital.

It was Saturday night, and the pub was full of army, navy and air-force men and women. Isaac played and the customers sang. As Vinnie collected an empty glass from a nearby table, Isaac rose from the piano stool and said with a wink, 'Vinnie, how about you play?'

'Me?'

'Come on, you can do *Bless 'em All*.'

So Vinnie sat and started to play and the customers began to sing with him. With this support, his confidence grew. He gave them 'Kiss Me Goodnight, Sergeant Major', followed by 'Daisy, Daisy'. The customers applauded and an air-force sergeant gave him a shilling. Vinnie would always remember that magical night.

* * *

And he'd never forget another date: Saturday 7th September, 1940. Mr Rosen asked him to deliver a message to an office in the West End that morning. Vinnie had to go on a tram, then a bus to Trafalgar Square. He found the office nearby and waited for the reply to Mr Rosen's message, then set off back to the pub.

He was only two streets away when the air-raid siren sounded – a mournful, tuneless wail that rose in pitch only to drop again, then rise once more. Vinnie had heard it often enough, but that had been during drills to get people used to them. He hurried on, hoping to reach the pub before anything happened. Then he heard the German bombers almost directly overhead. Their engines made a strange sound – a rising and falling note, not like the British planes. He could see the pub, where Mr Rosen would be inside waiting for his reply.

'Hey, you!' An air-raid warden in a steel helmet with 'ARP' on the front waved an angry arm. 'Bloody young fool! Get into the shelter!'

'I'm just going there, to the pub.' Vinnie pointed.

'Take shelter. Right now!'

Vinnie turned, then sprinted away from the pub and found the air-raid shelter. It was a squat, flat-roofed structure, built of bricks. Inside it was crowded with anxious people and the air was already heavy with fear. Some people cried; one man had bitten his bottom lip so hard the blood flowed. There were no seats left, so Vinnie sat cross-legged on the concrete floor between an old man and a young woman who hugged herself and muttered prayers. Overhead, the German bombers continued to drone.

'Hear that?' the old man asked no one in particular. 'That's them. The Jerries.' He kept time with the sound of the planes: '*Voom-ah, voom-ah, voom-ah.*'

'Will you shut up!' the young woman yelled. 'We can hear them and don't need your racket.'

'All right, keep your hair on.' The old man folded his arms in a sulky way.

Just then came: CRUMP, CRUMP, **CRUMP!** Three bombs in quick succession, coming frighteningly close. With each explosion, the ground shook. Dust and chips fell from the ceiling. Everyone in the shelter gasped at the same time. Vinnie held his breath, waiting for the fourth bomb, but it didn't come. The lights faltered, then went bright again. The aircraft moved on, fading into silence.

The young woman said, 'Maybe they've gone. Do you think?' In answer came a fresh wave of bombers, droning closer, then once more: CRUMP, CRUMP, **CRUMP!**

'That's the docks copping it,' the old man whispered, and this time no one told him to shut up. Someone sobbed. Everyone waited for that fourth bomb, but it didn't come – at least not on the shelter.

They stayed like that through the long night, silent at first, then gradually opening up and talking to each other. Neighbour found neighbour and gained comfort. Vinnie wished he'd brought his harmonica; then he could have given them a tune, the way Isaac did in the pub. After an age, the 'all clear' siren sounded, a welcome, long continuous note that seemed more cheerful because of what it meant. People in the shelter rose stiffly and stumbled outside, dazed and disbelieving, not understanding what had happened.

Where there had been tall buildings, there was a broken landscape. Vinnie could now see all the way to the cranes and the masts of ships in the docks. There was a dust haze everywhere, fires and smoke, bricks spilled over the streets, scattered roof slates and splintered timber jutting out at crazy angles.

The pub, when Vinnie found the place, was gone, smashed to a jumble of masonry. People could only gaze at the wreckage all around them. Vinnie recognised a pub customer, a man who worked in the docks.

'Vic, have you seen Isaac?' he asked. 'Or Mr and Mrs Rosen?'

'No mate.' Vic shook his head. 'But that was one bloody good pub.'

* * *

Vinnie watched rescue workers ease their way through the rubble, tossing bricks aside. Then came the bodies: one by one they were brought out, as if in slow motion. Each was covered with a grey blanket and gently carried away on a stretcher. By now, every rescuer's face was a mask of dust, but many of them had pink tear-marks running down their cheeks. Vinnie's face was powdered, too, and if he had a mirror, he'd have seen those same sorrowful lines. But in such a bombardment, neither mirror nor human being could remain unbroken.

He counted six bodies from the pub. Then the rescue workers packed up and headed off to another scene of destruction.

Vinnie kicked something at his feet. His harmonica. Somehow it had been blown out of the upstairs bedroom, to land here.

It was all there was left of his life in the pub; of his time of belonging with Mr and Mrs Rosen and Isaac. Vinnie wiped off the dust and was about to blow into it to see if it had survived the air raid when a voice shouted, 'Stop right there, boy!'

Vinnie froze. He faced a burly man in a dark-blue siren suit and a steel helmet with the word 'POLICE' stencilled on the front.

'Looting, are you?' the policeman demanded. 'Looting's a serious offence in wartime. Stealing from dead people, that's what it is.' His face grew red with anger. 'Scum of the earth, are looters. Scum of the earth!'

Express

ay 31, 1940

One Penny

nells the B.E.F. is crossing
story's strangest armada

OUSANDS
ALREADY

ought back to Dunkirk, aided by anes. British troops held the left oops the right flank. Last rear-

guard action (see inset) fought by French under General Prioux on the hills between Cassel and Ypres.

ty, hungry
y came back
unbeatable

Grac:
goes
Ameri

WITH a red, white
rosette in her
coat, Gracie Fields
husband Monty Banks
America last night
north-west port.

They announced on Tu
they were going. Then a
afterwards Monty Banks
am not going now."
closest friends knew
changed their minds agai
Gracie refused to be ph

STOP PR

FRENCH SAVE P
FOR COUNTER A
—Russian

Russian military exper
from Moscow last nig
French counter-attack wh
being planned will take p
Rethel area. For this cou
French are keeping h
planes.

"This is very noticeable
British air force is no
engaged in intense air
battle in Flanders. Su
British air force have
considerable in relation
numbers."

Signposts
to be
removed

SIR JOHN REITH, Minister of

and did not come on dec

Chapter Three
OUT OF LONDON

It was a little thing, the harmonica, and definitely Vinnie's legal property. No question. If he'd picked up *Isaac's* harmonica, then that could be looting. Vinnie tried to explain the difference, but the policeman would have none of it. It seemed he was angry about the German bombing and wanted to take it out on someone, anyone.

'Just you wait here, boy.' The policeman didn't hide his disgust. 'We caught another two of your lot, and you're all in trouble.' A black police van came slowly towards the corner where the pub had stood, the driver steering carefully around the rubble in the road. Vinnie's policeman called to the van driver: 'Got another one here. Caught red-handed.'

'Look, I'm not a looter.' Vinnie showed the harmonica. 'This is mine. Honest. I lived in the pub, worked there.'

'Prove it,' the policeman demanded.

Desperately, Vinnie looked around for a pub customer who'd recognise him as belonging to this place, but there was no one. The driver of the van was already out, opening the back door, ready to transport another offender to the police station. Then Vinnie remembered Mr Rosen's message. He said, 'Yesterday I went up the West End, with a letter from Mr Rosen. Here's the answer.'

The policeman tore open the envelope and read the contents. He shook his head. Now he was sympathetic. 'Well, you won't be delivering it, will you, lad?'

'No.' Vinnie could barely comprehend the flattened ruins of the pub and the terrible way death had come, the speed of it. There were things he still had to say to people. Before he'd left to deliver Mr Rosen's message, he'd been telling Isaac a story about his time with Aunty Vera and had said, in a casual way, 'Tell you the rest when I get back.' Now he was back, and there was no one to listen.

'And that was your home, eh?' The policeman sounded more kindly. 'So hop in the van, son, and we'll take you to a rest centre.'

Vinnie wasn't quick enough to say he had an uncle in Mile End or somewhere, and that he'd go there instead. He simply went where they put him.

The only good thing was that they let him ride in the front of the police van. He'd have hated to travel with the scum of the earth.

* * *

Rest centres had been set up as places where bombed-out people could stay until they gathered themselves and found somewhere else. The nearest one was at the town hall, not far from the pub. A harassed official took one look at Vinnie and said, 'A homeless boy? No parents, eh? He can be evacuated. Let's see, Euston Station. There's a train at eleven.' It was like he was ticking things off a list.

And that was it. In Vinnie's short journey to the town hall, he'd had time to collect his wits. He didn't want to be evacuated anywhere. The only place to be was the pub, not that it would do any good. It was gone; *they* were gone. But he'd rather be there than anywhere else. He could stay around for a while, look at the destruction, take things in, think about his lost friends and remember them. Always that. There would be funerals, too; he wanted to be there and be close to them. Say goodbye. Shed some tears. Who cared who saw them fall? All of that *had* to be done; *then* he'd think about his own life. Vinnie said to the official, 'Look, I know where Euston Station is. I can go there myself. Right?'

'No, sonny, that won't do. We've got a few other evacuees here. A bus will take the lot of you. Go and get yourself a sandwich and a cup of tea. Over there.'

A long trestle table had been set up with a tea urn at one end and plates of sandwiches in the middle. Two Women's Voluntary Service ladies in their grey uniforms handed out cups of tea. Dusty people took them in a dazed sort of way. Some didn't say thanks, or bother with sugar or milk. One or two didn't even touch the tea, but just held the cup in their hand. With their lives changed forever, who could eat and drink?

The town hall was filling up with people, but few of them spoke. Normally there'd be chatter and laughter in such a crowd, but not here. They just sat or stood around and looked blank. One woman nursed a large, grey cat and tried to feed him bits of sandwich. When Vinnie caught her eye, she whispered, 'He's all I've got. It's just us two now.'

'Make sure you hang on to him,' he said, then wandered on. The wall behind the trestle table was covered in posters from the government. One of them showed an air-raid warden saying to a small boy, 'Leave this to us, sonny – *you* ought to be out of London.'

Vinnie thought, *That's what they're doing. Treating me as a 'sonny' and sending me away from where I need to be.*

* * *

The next few hours passed in a blur; then Vinnie found himself trailing a bunch of other children along the tearful length of Platform Four.

He'd been to a railway station only once before, and it hadn't been Euston. One August before his mum died, they'd gone to Southend for a week at the seashore. That time, the station had been full of people going on holiday, bubbling with excitement. *Not much of that here*, Vinnie thought.

The whole place was full of children of every age and size. Many were openly crying, carrying cardboard gas-mask boxes and hugging small suitcases as if they were the most precious things they'd ever owned. Almost every boy or girl had a cardboard label tied to them with their name on it. A few children had come with their parents, which seemed to make things worse. Small boys and girls clung to their mothers. There were few fathers around. Even some porters and railway-station workers were stiff-jawed with the misery that was all around them.

Vinnie knew that trains from Euston Station went to the north-west of Britain, but that was about all he knew. Walking along the line of carriages on Platform Four, he found an open door, took a deep breath and climbed aboard.

There were two boys already in the compartment – both rich kids, he could tell. They wore round school caps, and blazers with a golden badge and Latin words on the pocket. The boys were deep in conversation, comparing notes about their different schools. They glanced up when Vinnie closed the carriage door behind him.

'I say, do leave the door open,' one of the boys said. 'It's so beastly stifling in here.' His cardboard label said his name was Ralph DuPreis.

'Yeah, sure.' Vinnie let the door swing open. He sat at one of the window seats, looking back along the platform at the unhappy stream of children boarding the train.

With that interruption sorted out, Ralph DuPreis ignored Vinnie and went on with what he'd been saying: 'And they're making our school into a hospital. The cricket pitch is to be the car park. I ask you. It's been played on since the eighteenth century. Lovely pitch. Bally waste if you ask me.' He sighed. 'Horrid.'

'Yes,' the other boy added, 'it's a dashed shame.'

Vinnie thought, *The stick of German bombs that flattened the pub and street and killed dozens, that was a dashed shame.* But he said nothing.

Just then he saw the girl with the distracted mother, Kathleen, coming along the platform. She held hands with her little brother, Joey, who kept faltering and looking back. Vinnie heard him ask, 'Kathleen, isn't Mummy coming to say goodbye to us?'

'She already did, Joey, back at the gate, so come on. Don't fuss. Please.' Kathleen reached Vinnie's compartment. The door was still open; in fact, it was the only one still open, as almost all the other carriages had filled with children by now. 'In you go, Joey,' she said. 'Step up.'

It seemed as if the little boy had lost everything in the world. Vinnie knew that look; it was all over the station. If you wanted more, a glance in the mirror was all it would take. And it was good to feel sorry for someone else. It made his own pain less. Vinnie rose from his seat. 'Why don't you sit here, Joey? Maybe you can see your mum back there. Give her a wave, eh?'

Without a word, Joey took Vinnie's seat and Kathleen followed her brother into the compartment. 'Thanks.' She put their suitcases and gas masks up in the luggage rack, then took the opposite window seat.

Kathleen had dark hair to her shoulders and wore a round school hat with a ribbon on it. Vinnie thought she looked quite nice – the only word he had for girls. At his school, if you said any more they'd think you were soppy. He sat beside Joey and said, 'Sister and brother? It's good you can be together.'

'It's something,' Kathleen agreed.

Ralph DuPreis regarded Joey and his sister as if they were interlopers. He soon returned to his conversation with the other boy. 'So why's *your* school being closed?'

'They're turning it into a billet of some kind,' the boy explained. 'Barracks for French refugees.'

'M-mm.' Ralph gave a small chuckle. 'My father says refugees are all right – in their own country.'

His friend snorted in amusement. Kathleen gave them a sharp look, which they ignored.

Isaac was a refugee. He was all right in his own country, or out of it. But he was not all right now. Never would be.

Another boy came striding along the platform and tossed a soft bag in through the open door. 'Got room for a little one?' The joke was that he was very tall and appeared to be all arms and legs. 'Dobbs is the name, evacuation's the game,' he quipped like a music-hall comedian. Without having to reach, he put his bag on the luggage rack, then folded himself into a seat beside Kathleen.

A porter came along, slamming carriage doors; then the guard's whistle sounded at the rear of the train.

'I can't see her,' Joey fretted. 'I can't see Mummy.'

'You will,' Kathleen assured him. 'Just as soon as soon. Mum'll visit us. She promised.'

There came a hiss of steam from the engine, and slowly the train began to move.

'I wonder where we'll end up?' Dobbs asked.

'Somewhere in the north, I heard. My name's Vinnie Cartwright.'

'Dobbs Stefanski. Short for Dobroslaw. A mouth-ful, eh?'

'I'm Joey,' Joey told them. 'Joey's short for Joseph.'

'Thought it might be.' Vinnie nodded.

'What's Vinnie short for?' Joey asked. 'Is it vinegar?'

Kathleen said, 'Don't be rude, Joey.'

Vinnie grinned. 'It wasn't rude. A bit of fun, that's all. Right, Joey?'

Joey relaxed for the first time and said, 'I'm nine. Kathleen's twelve.' In the same breath he asked, 'Why aren't you wearing a label, Vinnie, like everyone else?'

'It fell off,' Vinnie lied. The truth was, he wouldn't be seen dead wearing a cardboard luggage label. It was like they were parcels being sent somewhere. Might as well write 'FRAGILE' as well. That's how most of the kids in Euston Station looked, if their tears and sobs were anything to go by.

Kathleen showed her label and said, 'Kathleen Pearson.'

Vinnie glanced at Ralph DuPreis and his chum, but they were not going to play this name-swapping game. *Suit yourselves*, Vinnie thought. He caught Kathleen's eye. She nodded and murmured, 'M-mm, quite stuffy in here.' Then she smiled at Vinnie.

Nice, he thought. It was the first smile he'd seen in a long time. The train gathered pace, taking them away from London, out past the suburbs, then who could say where.

CIVIL DEFENCE
WOMEN WANTED FOR
EVACUATION SERVICE
OFFER YOUR SERVICES
TO YOUR LOCAL COUNCIL
OR ANY BRANCH OF WOMEN'S VOLUNTARY SERVICES

Chapter Four
THERE

Joey asked, 'Are we there yet?'

'Joey, we don't even know where *there* is,' Kathleen answered. 'So let's wait and see.' They'd done a slow hour of stop-start travelling with few words said between them.

Joey gazed out of the window as the train rolled through a small station. 'This place is called Nowhere,' he reported, 'because it's got no name.'

'No, silly,' Ralph DuPreis spoke up at last. 'All station names have been taken away in case German spies use them to work out where they are.'

Kathleen flared up: 'It wasn't silly. It was just a remark! Nothing silly about it.'

'Give him a chance,' Vinnie said. 'He's only nine.'

'I'm just pointing out the facts.'

Vinnie responded, 'So point them out the window.'

'Hey, hey, what's this?' Dobbs butted in. 'Why the aggravation all of a sudden? I thought we were at war with old Hitler, not each other.'

'Everybody *knows* about station names being removed,' Ralph persisted. 'It was in the *Daily Telegraph*.'

'Well, that proves it.' Dobbs folded his arms and shook his head from side to side. 'That jolly well proves it.'

'Is that a mouth organ?' Kathleen pointed to the silvery flash sticking out of Vinnie's breast pocket.

'Harmonica.' Vinnie took it out.

Joey brightened and asked, 'Can you play *Ten Green Bottles*?'

'Sure,' said Vinnie, and began to play.

Ralph folded his arms and exchanged looks with his chum from the posh school that would soon be a billet for French refugees. Their expressions showed lofty disdain.

Kathleen and Joey began to sing. When the last green bottle had fallen from the wall, Dobbs said, 'And now, I give it to you in Polish. Music, maestro, please.'

There was laughter as Dobbs sang the verses using what he said were Polish words. It sounded something like: *Dziesiec zielonych butelek wiszacych na scianie.*

Kathleen and Joey tried to join in, but the pronunciation was tricky and there were too many syllables in the Polish version to fit the tune.

'Okay, Ralphie,' Vinnie challenged, 'How about you give it to us in Latin?'

'I think not.' Ralph crossed his legs and looked out of the window.

Vinnie shrugged and began to play 'One Man Went to Mow'. Then he stopped, held up one finger and said, 'Listen.'

Half-a-dozen small voices in the next compartment had taken up the song.

Dobbs remarked, 'Catching, eh?'

'You've started something,' Kathleen said. After a pause she added, 'Vinnie.'

* * *

Playing the simple, familiar tunes had taken Vinnie's mind off his sadness. The locomotive started slowing down, then pulled into a small country station where it shunted back and forth for several busy minutes before coupling up to the rest of the carriages and steaming away into the distance. They had been disconnected from the train and were left in silence.

After a minute, Joey whispered, 'We've been abandoned.'

'Marooned in the middle of nowhere,' Dobbs added.

'Another engine will come for us,' Kathleen assured Joey, but still they sat.

It was Ralph who stood up and said to his chum, 'Shall we stretch our legs?'

'Yes, let's.' Without another word Ralph opened the compartment door on their side and strode out onto the platform.

As they moved away from the carriage, Ralph added, 'I say, what a dashed relief.'

Kathleen looked at the open door. 'We might as well take a look. What do you think? There should be a toilet here.'

'And a drink of water,' Joey added as they left the compartment.

'Water, water!' Dobbs clutched his throat, pretending to be overcome with thirst. 'Give me water.' He staggered out after Kathleen and Joey, wobbling on his long legs as he went.

Along the carriage, other evacuees began to open their doors and step out onto the platform, cautiously, as if some overbearing adult might appear and order them back again. But they were left in peace to explore the station, not that there was much to see: a few milk churns and a baggage trolley with nothing on it.

Vinnie stayed alone in the compartment and let the memories flood back, every one full of pain and loss. The air raid, the destruction and what he'd seen there in its midst. The 'scum of the earth' remark, the rest centre, then the misery of Euston Station;

one hurt piled on another. He no longer belonged in London, nor here, and probably not where he was going either.

He remembered a morning in the upstairs bedroom. It had been early, about a quarter to five. Isaac was up and dressed, while Vinnie still lay curled in his blanket.

'Come on, Vinnie,' Isaac had said. 'Out of bed.'

'Another five minutes. Please. I don't feel like playing this morning.'

'Sometimes musicians don't feel like it either. But they do it. It's what makes them musicians.'

So Vinnie had got up, dressed, splashed some water on his face and gone downstairs to the piano, where Isaac said, 'If you want something, you must work for it.'

In his lonely railway-carriage compartment, Vinnie thought now, *Even if that something is wanting to belong?*

He stepped out onto the platform. Further along, in a patch of sunshine, two small girls had a length of skipping rope that they turned between them. Dobbs was already in the middle, galumphing awkwardly, ducking his head because the girls couldn't swing the rope high enough. He chanted as he jumped: 'Salt, pepper, vinegar, mustard. Salt, pepper, vinegar, mustard.'

Joey and some of the other evacuee boys and girls clapped their hands in time to the rope. Kathleen was smiling. When Vinnie approached, she said,

'The toilets are just there, Vinnie. And a water fountain.'

'Thanks, Kathleen.'

* * *

They stayed half an hour in that station; then a smaller locomotive came and was coupled up to their single carriage. A porter suddenly appeared from the ticket office and ushered them into their compartments; he closed all the doors and they were off again, but no longer on the main line.

Some time later, the one-carriage train came to a stop with a squeal of brakes. An elderly porter began opening compartment doors, calling out, 'Netterfold, this is Netterfold Station.'

Dobbs announced, 'Looks like this is it, folks. We're here.'

Joey said, 'Thanks for the music, Vinnie.'

'It was very good,' Kathleen added. 'Cheered us up.'

'You're welcome,' Vinnie said. 'Any time.'

Kathleen stepped out of the compartment and Joey followed. Like a seasoned traveller, Ralph DuPreis gathered a pigskin suitcase from the overhead luggage rack, then pushed past Vinnie and stepped out onto the platform too.

'Excuse me.' Ralph's still nameless friend left the compartment next, stepping out along the platform as if this were something he did every day.

He caught up with Ralph, exchanged a word. They moved off together, laughing.

Ralph's friend carried his gas mask in a neat leather holder. Most people made do with the cardboard box their mask came in, hanging it from their shoulder with a string. Vinnie didn't have a gas mask, but everyone else did. Come to that, he didn't have anything at all, except a harmonica. He'd left London in such a rush, without clothes or pyjamas to sleep in. Or money. If he'd thought more clearly in the rest centre, he could have asked someone about it.

'I've never heard of this place,' Dobbs observed as he stepped out onto the platform. 'Are we in England, Wales or Scotland?' He waited by the open door.

'Don't know,' Vinnie answered. Then it happened.

Dobbs said, 'Are you coming?' He added his name: 'Vinnie?'

'Yeah,' Vinnie agreed. He left the compartment and joined Dobbs.

Kathleen had waited for them outside, with Joey. 'Shall we four keep together?'

Suddenly Vinnie felt better.

✱ ✱ ✱

At the station exit a woman called, 'Welcome, boys and girls. Welcome, welcome.' She wore the Women's Voluntary Service uniform. 'Now, come along this way, please. Mr Preston is waiting outside for you in his bus.'

Vinnie made sure Kathleen, Joey and Dobbs were with him; then they moved through the station exit together.

The bus outside was an old one. Mr Preston sat at the wheel, looking surly. The evacuee children climbed aboard and sat nursing their cases. Vinnie counted fifteen evacuees who'd arrived on the train, excluding Ralph and his chum, who weren't on the bus.

'Come on, you lot,' Mr Preston growled. 'I don't have all day.' He started the engine and moved off before Dobbs had sat down.

'Watch it, squire!' Dobbs stumbled and landed heavily in the seat next to Vinnie.

'You got a precious cargo here,' Vinnie added.

Mr Preston ignored this and kept driving, hunched over the wheel. He was a young man, maybe twenty or so, which was strange because since the war had begun it was women who drove buses, or older men. *You look young and fit enough to be in the army*, Vinnie thought. *Are you a draft dodger? Conscientious objector? Is that what's making you so bad-tempered – folks having a go at you all the time?* In any case, Vinnie concluded, Mr Preston's attitude was not doing the evacuees any good. *So Mr Preston, you might as well have stayed home.* He hoped they'd get a warmer reception from the other people they met in this town.

The slow bus journey took them through quiet country lanes, past fields of grazing cows and sheep. It was very pretty, Vinnie decided, like a country scene in the 1939 calendar that used to hang in the butcher's shop near the pub. They rolled into the village, where a group of kids, about six of them, stepped back from the roadside to let the bus pass. One tall boy with red hair shook his fist at the evacuees and shouted something.

Kathleen recoiled. 'What did he say?'

'I don't think it was, *Welcome to Netterfold*,' Vinnie muttered.

'He shook his fist at us!' Joey said.

Dobbs suggested, 'Maybe it's a local custom.'

The bus pulled in at a village hall, and Mr Preston just nodded in the direction of the building. 'Right. In there, you lot.'

The evacuees scrambled off the bus and made their way uneasily into the hall. No one spoke or made eye contact.

Inside, they found tables on which a smiling vicar and his wife had laid out plates of sandwiches, one jug of milk and another of very pale orange juice. 'Grub,' Joey whispered to Kathleen. 'Should we just help ourselves?'

'Better wait until we're invited. And it's not grub. It's food.'

'Tastes the same as grub,' Vinnie said. 'Unless Mr Preston put a curse on it.'

The WVS woman who'd greeted them at the

station bustled in and raised her hands for silence. 'I'm Mrs Ormsby-Chapman, and I'm sure you'd all like something to fill your raging tummies, so do tuck in, children – but remember there are food shortages, so please only take what you can eat. Then we'll see about your billets.'

And who should have come into the hall behind Mrs Ormsby-Chapman, but Ralph DuPreis and his friend? At this, Vinnie shook his head and muttered, 'What was wrong with the bus?' But nobody heard him. The evacuees had already moved towards the tables, because many of them hadn't eaten since breakfast. He followed the others.

Joey asked, 'What's a billet?'

'It's a bit of wood,' Kathleen answered.

'Yeah, about that size.' Dobbs held his hands apart to show how long.

Vinnie remembered the conversation on the train, about one of the posh schools being turned into a billet – barracks for French refugees. He said, 'No, I think it's the place where we'll stay.'

Mrs Ormsby-Chapman went on to explain that they'd be looked after by foster-parents, who would arrive presently. 'So just wait there, girls and boys,' she instructed them, then turned away to talk importantly with another woman.

Vinnie thought, *Here we go again.*

Chapter Five
THE LAST PUPPY
IN THE PET SHOP

Ralph DuPreis and his friend made a point of ignoring the sandwiches.

'How'd they get here?' Joey whispered to Dobbs.

'It wasn't a taxi.' Dobbs didn't care who heard. 'Not in this place.'

'I expect they came in Mrs Ormsby-Chapman's car,' Kathleen sniffed, and Vinnie liked her even more. Dobbs and Joey, too.

He stood with them watching the selection process happen. It was a peculiar way of going on, he thought, starting when a majestic-looking woman sailed into the hall like some grand ocean-liner docking at Tilbury. She had to be someone important in the village. Her ladyship wore a tweed skirt, a fox fur round her shoulders and a long feather in her hat. Straight away she took a fancy to Ralph DuPreis and he took a liking to her. She smiled down and he smiled up; she murmured a few words to him, and Vinnie heard Ralph answer, 'Yes, ra-ther!' Then off they went, both well pleased with their choice of each other.

'Looks like he's all right,' Kathleen whispered.

Dobbs added, 'And they all lived happily ever after.'

Joey said, 'Amen.'

'Don't say that, Joey,' Kathleen scolded.

Joey fired back, 'You can say things about him, why can't I?'

'Because I'm older,' she answered.

Somehow all four of them realised that to be well chosen, you had to look right.

Ralph's mate was next to go. Mrs Ormsby-Chapman had picked the boy out and kept him close at hand until a second woman entered the hall. She was less grand than the one who'd taken Ralph, and didn't wear a fox fur or feathered hat. But she spoke nicely. Almost at once she weighed up Ralph's mate and breathed, 'Oh, yes.' After a few enthusiastic words between them, they left the hall chatting as if they'd known each other forever.

Where Vinnie had lived in London, few people were better off than their neighbour. No one had more money, more possessions or better prospects than anyone else. And Vinnie had never felt envy.

Everyone was in the same boat, except Aunty Vera, who'd made herself a cut above most people. But they knew Vera. 'Lady Muck' is what they called her – more *lah-di-dah* than the Queen.

It was well known there were toffs and nobs, wealthy people, who lived in the country or the better-off parts of London. Few of Vinnie's lot ever went to those parts of London, unless it was to do a bit of work, like clearing a blocked drain or shifting some furniture. ('Ta, guv'nor. Much obliged.') Mind you, there were some who went there *without* invitation, usually in the dead of night for a spot of thieving.

So Vinnie had never had anything to do with the upper class until now. And what he'd just witnessed didn't make him envious – far from it. If that was how they stuck together, they were welcome to each other.

Then the ordinary foster-parents were allowed into the hall. They entered together, as if they'd been queuing outside. Some smiled and talked to the children straight away, but others cast their eyes around shrewdly, saying nothing. One woman approached Vinnie's group, moving slowly with arms folded across her chest, handbag dangling from its strap on her shoulder. She weighed all four of them up, then confronted Kathleen: 'Brother and sister, are you?'

'Yes, we are.'

'And staying together.' Joey moved closer to Kathleen.

The woman sniffed. 'M-mm. I'm really looking for two girls. And a bit older.'

'Sorry, love,' Vinnie said, talking like a market stallholder, 'we ain't got any your size.'

The woman ignored him and moved on. Kathleen whispered, 'This is horrible.'

Joey added, 'It's like a slave market. Remember that story Mum read us?'

'Mum read *you* the story, Joey, not me.'

'Do you think we'll have to work in our billets?' Joey said in a small voice.

'Nah, we'll be fine,' Dobbs assured him. 'And it's not a slave market, Joey. Leastways, they're not *paying* for us.'

Now that Vinnie could see the other evacuees properly, he noticed that one or two were poorly dressed and none too clean. The foster-parents passed the scruffy ones quickly; maybe giving a smile or asking what their name was, or where they came from, although everyone knew the answer was London. Vinnie guessed they wanted to know which *part* of London. The cleaner, better-dressed evacuees were first to go.

The handbag woman chose a small girl in a pixie hood and grubby skirt with stains on it. The woman remarked to another, 'On the way home I'll stop off at the chemist. Get something for her hair. You know – *lice*.' Then she left the hall and the girl followed meekly. She'd heard every word her new foster-parent had said.

Next it was Dobbs Stefanski's turn to go. A short, but pleasant-looking woman shielded her eyes with a hand, gazed at his height and said, 'Well, you're a lofty one, and no mistake. What's it like up there?'

'Elevated,' he said.

'You'll be handy in my shop. Get things down from high shelves. So would you like to come with me, then?'

Dobbs gave Vinnie, Kathleen and Joey a who-can-help-it shrug and murmured, 'So long, see you sometime.' Then he went off with the woman, who asked his name and said kindly as they left the hall, 'Was it a long journey, then?'

Joey watched them enviously. 'Why can't we go with that lady?'

'We don't get to choose, Joey,' Kathleen responded. 'They do.'

'Hullo, you two are to come with me.' A sharp-voiced woman stood a little distance away, looking Kathleen and Joey up and down as if measuring them for something. 'The pair of you will do very well in my house. There's only me and my son, Dennis. He works on the railway, in a reserved occupation.'

Kathleen and Joey picked up their suitcases and gas masks and followed the woman to the door, then both turned and gave Vinnie a resigned sort of wave. Kathleen asked the woman, 'May Joey and I know your name, please?'

'Oh, nice manners.' The woman was impressed. 'I'm Mrs Watney. Did you bring your ration books?'

As the afternoon wore on, all the other evacuees went away with foster-parents, leaving Vinnie on his own. Mrs Ormsby-Chapman kept reassuring him that someone would come soon. More time passed, and Vinnie sensed she was losing confidence about anyone else turning up. He was too, but he tried not to show any concern. From time to time, the woman conferred in a hushed voice with two other WVS women. The shrug of their shoulders plainly said: *What are we going to do with him tonight?*

Don't worry, ladies, Vinnie thought, *I don't want to be stuck with you any more than you want to be lumbered with me.*

'Won't be long now,' Mrs Ormsby-Chapman said brightly for the fifth time.

At that moment, the hall door opened and another woman came in, looking flustered. 'Am I too late?'

'No, no, not at all, Mrs Greenwood.' Mrs Ormsby-Chapman hid her relief. 'This one is called Vinnie Cartwright.' She added, 'The last puppy in the pet shop.'

As he left the hall with Mrs Greenwood, Vinnie felt like saying, 'Woof, woof!' Then cocking a leg and pretending to pee against the doorpost. That'd teach them.

*   *   *

Meanwhile, on the outskirts of town, Kathleen and Joey had discovered that Mrs Watney's house had three storeys and stood apart from its neighbours.

As they walked, she said to Joey, 'Now, young man, are you dry at night?'

Joey didn't understand. 'Do you mean, do I get thirsty?'

Kathleen came to his aid. 'Joey's very good. Has been for years.'

'I like to know these things,' Mrs Watney said. 'I can't be washing bedsheets all the time.'

They reached the house and Mrs Watney opened the door for them.

Kathleen and Joey were to share a bedroom at the top of the house. It had a sloping ceiling with a skylight window, which was covered with thick black paper. The only daylight came through the open door to the hallway. There were two single beds, each with a quilt made of stitched-together squares of different material. The room also had a cupboard with some wooden coathangers inside. Mrs Watney instructed, 'The lavatory's one floor down, and there's a chamber-pot under the bed. Make sure you empty it in the morning and rinse it out. We don't want any disease here. You get a bath once a week and you share the water, one after the other, of course – and don't fill the bath more than four inches.'

'Yes, Mrs Watney,' Kathleen agreed. The advertisement for Pears soap said it could be *five* inches! But never mind.

'Tea's at half-past five, and you'll eat in the kitchen with Dennis and I,' Mrs Watney went on. 'And you're not to waste food.'

The list went on: they could have the gaslight on

in the bedroom, but it was to be out by half-past eight. Kathleen and Joey already knew about the black-out, from London. No one was allowed to show a light from a window or doorway at night, in case it was seen by a German bomber. There were no streetlights, and cars, lorries and buses had hoods over their headlamps. Some people bought luminous flowers to wear at night so they could be seen walking along the street. The blackout caused dozens of accidents.

'Now,' Mrs Watney finished her introduction, 'I'll let you settle in. You can bring the ration books when you come downstairs.' She gave a final suspicious look around, then stumped off down the hall.

Joey said in a voice of dismay, 'This is the horriblest wicked-witch story there ever was.'

'At least we've got a potty,' Kathleen pointed out. 'That's something, isn't it?'

Joey sat on one of the beds and folded his arms. 'I hate Adolf Hitler. Bet *he* doesn't sleep in a place like this.'

'And I bet *he* wets his bed,' Kathleen added firmly. Joey caught Kathleen's eye and she smiled. In this war, making jokes about Adolf Hitler was all that children could do.

* * *

As Vinnie walked with Mrs Greenwood, she explained, 'You'll stay at Netterfold House, Vinnie. I'm Miss Armstrong's housekeeper. She keeps to herself.'

'But I'll meet her?'

'It's not likely. She made room for you, but that's as much as she'll do.'

'Then how can I say thanks?' Vinnie persisted. 'I mean, I'd have to, wouldn't I?'

'There's no need. Miss Armstrong's done her bit—'

At that moment, a group of local boys barged out of a shop doorway. They swung in behind Vinnie, calling in turn, 'There goes another one! Taking over the place.'

'Yeah, bloody vaccies. Took our school bus. We had to walk home.'

'Go back where you came from. Coward! Running away from a few old bombs.'

'Why are you giving *him* house room, missus?'

The boys began to chant, 'Vaccy coward! Vaccy coward!'

Mrs Greenwood turned to face the tallest boy, who had pushed forward from the group. 'Freddie Preston, stop being such a child.' Vinnie recognised him as the red-headed local he'd seen from the bus window.

The local boys broke off their chant, but they still muttered and jeered. Mrs Greenwood and Vinnie walked on, but Freddie Preston had a final jibe: 'You'll be murdered in your bed, missus. You'll see. Except you *won't* see, 'cause you'll be dead.'

Vinnie remembered what Dobbs had said on the train: 'I thought we were at war with old Hitler.'

* * *

The kitchen of Netterfold House was a large room with a long wooden table taking up the middle. There were shelves on the walls and tidy racks of copper cooking pots and dishes. *How will I fit in here?* Vinnie wondered. Everything seemed to belong together. Take one thing away and it wouldn't look right.

Adolf took a lot of things away and now nothing looks right.

'I expect you've had quite a day, Vinnie,' Mrs Greenwood said. 'All that travelling and waiting around.'

And the bombs and the deaths. Voom-ah, voom-ah, CRUMP, CRUMP, CRUMP!

Tears came to his eyes as he stood there in the kitchen. Mrs Greenwood saw this and turned away to give him a moment.

Then from another part of the house came the gentle intrusion of someone playing a piano. Instantly, it carried Vinnie back to the smoky pub, with Isaac hunched over the keyboard. The hairs on the back of his neck bristled as the rippling music flowed through him. He closed his eyes, saw Isaac wringing his effortless beauty out of the old piano, talking as he played: 'This is a bit much for you, Vinnie.'

'I'd love to be able to play it.'

'Maybe one day. It's Schubert.'

'Schubert,' Vinnie said aloud now.

Mrs Greenwood's eyes lit up in surprise. 'You know it, then? Schubert?'

'Um – I've heard it before.'

'It's Miss Armstrong's gramophone. These days it's all she plays. Her records.' Mrs Greenwood ladled stew into a bowl. 'Come, sit down and eat. Poor soul, you look absolutely done in. This is rabbit,' she went on. 'You like rabbit?'

'Thanks, I eat anything,' Vinnie said.

Mrs Greenwood put the bowl on the table, then laid a gentle hand on his shoulder and squeezed. After that she left him in peace to listen to the music.

This place will do, he thought. *Even better if I can hear that gramophone properly.* It turned the local kids' insults into nothing; pushed away that picture of Ralph DuPreis at the head of the queue and the sad little girl with the dirty hair. It buried the hurt of being the last puppy in the pet shop. *With music like that, I don't care about any of them.*

* * *

Vinnie's bedroom had a chair, a small table with a light on it, and a narrow bed. Before saying good-night, he had thanked Mrs Greenwood for being kind. There would be a lot of 'thank you for this', 'much obliged for that'. It would come, he knew.

He lay in the darkness, listening for night sounds, but there was nothing: no dustbin lids being knocked off, cats yowling or happy, drunken merchant seamen singing their way back to their ships in the London docks. He thought about the city. *Is Hitler giving them hell tonight, raining bombs down on everybody?*

He slept.

Bless my life! what's this I see?
If it isn't a little EVACUEE
       Don't be afraid
              when it's dark at night
They simply can't put out my light.

Chapter Six
NETTERFOLD

Kathleen and Joey rose early, washed their faces and went downstairs. Mrs Watney was at the stove, pushing something to and fro in a black frying pan. She gave an unsmiling nod. 'So you're up, then?'

'Yes, good morning, Mrs Watney,' Kathleen said.

'Breakfast's just coming. Dennis already had his and went to work. You'll have to wait till this afternoon to meet him.'

'That'll be nice.'

At tea the night before, Dennis hadn't been there. Mrs Watney explained he'd had to do a late shift at the railway yard.

Breakfast was an omelette made out of dried

egg powder from a khaki packet. There was also toast and strawberry jam.

'Go easy on that,' Mrs Watney warned. 'Jam'll be rationed soon.' Then she turned and busied herself at the sink.

During the night in the darkened room upstairs, Kathleen had told Joey a story she'd made up about a gnome who was so tall none of the other gnomes wanted anything to do with him. Halfway through she'd realised he was asleep, and in that lonely moment a tear had come. *I'm not going to cry*, she'd told herself. *I'll save it for when something really terrible happens, and hope it never does.*

In the morning she'd woken suddenly, with no idea where she was. Then everything had come horribly rushing back. But thousands of evacuees were waking to that same feeling: a whole Euston Station full of them, and more.

At the breakfast table, Joey whispered to Kathleen, 'Go on, ask her.'

Mrs Watney noticed. 'What is this you're to ask me?'

Kathleen said, 'Mrs Watney, do you think Joey could listen to *Children's Hour*? On the wireless?'

'It's on the BBC,' Joey added. 'Five o'clock.'

'Don't see why not,' Mrs Watney agreed; then she said, 'Oh, but wait. The accumulator needs charging. Dennis could hardly hear his football on Saturday.'

The accumulator turned out to be a square glass battery with two connections on top. If Joey and

Kathleen liked, Mrs Watney said, they could take it to the garage and exchange it for a charged one. Kathleen jumped at the chance to get out of the house, and maybe find Vinnie and Dobbs.

Mrs Watney said, 'Don't forget you have to write to your mother. And leave the envelope open so I can pop a note in before I post it.'

They took the accumulator to the garage. Joey said, as they walked, 'If the envelope's open, she'll read what we write. We can't tell Mum how horrible it is.'

'Let's pretend it's not.'

Joey shrugged. 'So I'll use a secret code. Tell Mum that way.'

Kathleen shook her head. 'Now it means *I'll* have to read your letter.'

The man in Netterfold's garage was cheerful and gave them a fully charged accumulator. 'That'll be tuppence,' he said.

Kathleen paid. It was for a good cause.

* * *

Vinnie had a breakfast egg in the kitchen. A real one, not dried egg powder – a country egg with a brown shell. It was soft-boiled, so he could dip fingers of toast into it. There was tea as well, with honey to sweeten it and spread on the rest of his toast. Mrs Greenwood asked if he had a ration book.

'I never got one,' Vinnie explained. 'Sorry.' *Aunty Vera kept it. She's probably still using it.*

'I'll see to it,' Mrs Greenwood said. 'And what about your clothes?'

'My place was bombed,' Vinnie told her. 'They never gave me a chance to find my stuff.'

Mrs Greenwood shook her head, then bustled. 'There's some sort of emergency committee. I'll ask at the council.'

Vinnie said, 'Can I do some work around the place, Mrs Greenwood?'

'It's up to you, Vinnie. There's firewood to chop, and the garden needs attention. Mrs Hall's boy, Henry, used to come in, but he delivers telegrams now.'

So on his first morning in Netterfold House, Vinnie found an axe in the garden shed and began to chop some logs. Taking his feelings out on the firewood made him feel a little better, although the split logs flew off left and right, which only meant he had to go and pick them up. When he didn't swing the axe so hard, there was less distance to travel.

The piano music started again, and with the firewood stacked in the shed, Vinnie quietly moved around the house. He soon found the window that was closest to the sound. Nearby were garden beds full of plants that looked like weeds. He knelt and spent a gentle hour working steadily and listening.

This became a two-hour job, with soothing Beethoven and Mozart for company.

'So here you are, then?' It was Mrs Greenwood. 'I came to say there's a biscuit in the kitchen, and a glass of milk.'

'Oh, thanks, Mrs Greenwood.' He could have done without the interruption, but the music stopped anyway.

'And after you've eaten, why don't you go for a walk, Vinnie? Have a look around the village. Maybe catch up with some of your friends.'

* * *

Now that Vinnie could examine Netterfold properly, he saw that parts of it looked like a picture postcard. There were low cottages and taller houses, some with ivy growing up the walls. It was very beautiful, Vinnie decided; very peaceful.

He walked on. There was nothing much in the main street apart from a group of shops, including a post office. Few cars and lorries moved about. Since petrol had been rationed, it was like that all over Britain.

Four young people his own age came towards him – three boys and one girl. Instantly Vinnie was on his guard. They were some of the locals who'd greeted the bus yesterday, then chanted after him when he walked to his billet with Mrs Greenwood. Freddie Preston led the way, walking chin-first like a boxer lining up for a fight.

There was a rule Vinnie had learned back in London: if you had to face trouble, get in first. He confronted Freddie.

'You got something to say to us?'

'Yeah.' Freddie thrust himself forward. 'Plenty.'

'There's more vaccies than there is of your lot,' Vinnie warned.

'Yeah,' Freddie scoffed. 'Some of your lot are just this size.' He demonstrated with a hand at his knee. 'And the rest are *girls*.'

Vinnie said, 'Some pretty *fierce* girls.' He was making this up.

Another boy, taller than Freddie, barged forward and snarled, 'Go back where you came from.' He pushed Vinnie hard, making him tumble backwards over a low wall, grazing his wrist.

The group walked on, the girl calling back: 'And don't even *think* about coming to our school.'

School, eh? I forgot about that. Vinnie nursed his injured wrist. There was blood showing. He took back what he'd decided about the place being beautiful and peaceful. Beauty was more than how things looked from the outside. And peace was something you made – only with that lot, it wasn't going to be easy.

* * *

Netterfold village had a small park with a swing and a roundabout. It was there that Vinnie found Kathleen and Joey.

'Vinnie!' Joey jumped off the swing and ran to meet him. 'We got shouted at.'

'By a bunch of stupid hooligans.' Kathleen was red in the face.

'Never mind,' Vinnie said. 'If they come to London, we'll fix them.'

Joey liked this idea. 'We'll get the beefeaters to prong them with pikes, then lock them in the Tower.'

'What's your place like, Vinnie?' Kathleen asked. 'Your billet?'

'Not bad,' Vinnie reported. 'Nice housekeeper. The lady who owns the place I've not, um, seen yet.'

'Our foster-mother is evil,' Joey said darkly. 'First thing she asked was did I wet the bed.'

'What a demon.' Vinnie shook his head at the boldness of the woman.

'Just for that,' Joey went on, 'I might start doing it. In earnest. I might stand up on the bedrail and let fly.'

'Joey!' Kathleen scolded. To Vinnie she said, 'He's missing Mum.'

Dobbs wandered into the park, raised a hand in greeting, then sat on the lowest swing so that his knees came up almost level with his ears. 'Not too bad so far,' he volunteered. 'My foster-mum's the postmistress, Mrs Hall. It's just her and her son, Henry, the telegram boy. He's a bit glum, so Mrs H does all the talking. She's full of news, so I don't need to turn on the wireless.'

Vinnie thought, *One ogre, one chatterbox and Miss A, who keeps to herself.*

'We're getting *Children's Hour* this afternoon.' Joey showed the accumulator. 'That's what this is for.'

'School starts on Monday.' Dobbs' expression had become gloomy. The rest of their faces fell.

'Freddie Preston's mob warned me not to go,' Vinnie told them. 'Is that a good enough excuse?'

'Maybe there's a different school for us,' Kathleen suggested.

'In a place this size?' Vinnie objected. 'Can't see it myself.'

'There's one bit of good news,' Joey announced. 'The man at the garage said the railway yard's down that way.' He pointed. 'So maybe I can watch trains and engines. I couldn't do that in London.'

'Glad somebody's happy,' Dobbs said.

'I didn't say I was happy. Only said they've got trains.'

They mooched about in the park a while longer, comparing notes and trying to cheer each other up. Then hunger drove them back to their billets.

* * *

Soon it was five o'clock and Joey came downstairs and switched on the wireless. Before long there came the comforting *Children's Hour* theme music. Joey smiled. He was among friends, for a short while anyway. Kathleen joined him.

The front door opened and a voice announced for the world to hear, 'It's me!'

'Oh, you're home early, love,' Mrs Watney greeted

the newcomer, who clumped into the kitchen. They talked loudly, not seeming to care that Joey and Kathleen were trying to listen to the wireless, which was an old one with occasional spits and crackles instead of voices and music.

The new arrival was Dennis. He looked to be about eighteen and wore dark-blue overalls and a railway-worker's cap. Dennis carried a metal sandwich box and a tea bottle, both of which Mrs Watney took from him. His face and his hands were black with coal-dust. He talked on loudly, ignoring Kathleen and Joey: 'I'm famished, Ma,' he said. 'Hope you've got something tasty. And lots of it.'

'You go and wash, son, and your tea will be on the table,' Mrs Watney told him. Dennis seemed to enjoy his mother's attention. 'Is this one of your nights out, Dennis, love?'

'Yes, Mum. I'll slip out a bit later. See what's what.'

'That's good, son.'

'And what have we got here?' Dennis turned at last to Kathleen and Joey, but asked the question of Mrs Watney. 'Is this the vaccies, then?'

'Yes, Kathleen's the girl, and Joey's her brother.' Mrs Watney put on a winning voice. 'Say hullo, kiddies, to my lovely son, Dennis.'

Kathleen and Joey both greeted Dennis, but he made no reply, except to ask his mother, 'And what's that they've got on?'

'I think it's *Children's Hour*, Dennis dear.'

'Well, I'm not having that kiddiewinks rubbish on while I'm eating my tea,' Dennis ruled. 'When I come down again, it goes off. Right?'

'I expect they'll have had enough of it by then, love,' Mrs Watney soothed him.

With that battle won, Dennis left the kitchen. Joey switched off the wireless, and without another word he and Kathleen went for a walk before tea.

'Can we go and see the railway yard?' Joey asked once they were outside.

'If you like.'

*　*　*

After having tea in the kitchen that evening, Vinnie went to his bedroom, took out his harmonica and started to play. It was a sweet melody he'd learned from Isaac. *Playing that tune, any tune*, he thought, *is the most cheering-up thing I can do. Close my eyes, and all this disappears. Keep them shut, and carry on playing; then I'm somewhere else, surrounded by my own people.*

The tune brought memories of his year with Isaac in the pub, where he'd learned more than just simple tunes, sweet though some of them were. Over those months, Vinnie had found himself becoming more patient, and gentler. It was the music that made him like that, always the music – either as he listened to Isaac at the piano or when he picked out a new piece by himself.

The old lady's gramophone records did it, too. He'd rage and hate; then with the first chords, he would calm down.

Vinnie played on, vowing not to cry over the tune, although it was sad as well as beautiful. With all those memories contained in the song, it was hard to get through.

Just then, there came a light knock on his bedroom door. It opened and a tall woman stood looking in. Vinnie sprang off the bed. He hid the harmonica behind his back. The woman in the doorway clutched a walking stick with fingers that were gnarled and twisted. She frowned as if there were a mystery to be solved and said, 'I heard music. Young man, was it you playing that music?'

5" of water... *(that's patriotism*

a tablet of WRIGHT'S
(that's practical

Gad sir ! They're right about Wright's. What a magnifice[nt]
lather with just a spot of warm water (or cold if you're
spartan). And what a clean job of work after a night on dut[y].
And what a fine reconditioning for another day's work.

WRIGHT'S Coal Tar Soap
$7\frac{1}{2}$D per tablet (Tax included) One tablet — one coupo[n]

Chapter Seven
BEAUTIFUL DREAMER

The woman had to be Miss Armstrong, Vinnie reasoned, the owner of Netterfold House. She was the one who'd taken him in, given him house room, and now he'd annoyed her, playing his harmonica when she wanted to listen to her gramophone records. 'Sorry, ma'am,' he mumbled. 'I didn't mean any harm.'

'You must never apologise for making music; only for making bad music – which you weren't. We haven't met yet, I'm Lila Armstrong. I do hope you are settling in.'

'I am, thank you, ma'am. And my name's Vinnie Cartwright.'

'Yes, I learned that from Mrs Greenwood.' Miss

Armstrong sounded strict, like a teacher, except she had a gleam in her eyes. She asked, 'Now, before I came in, what were you playing?'

'Um – this, ma'am.' Vinnie showed her the harmonica.

'No, not the instrument.' Miss Armstrong hid a smile. 'I mean, what tune?'

'Oh.' Vinnie understood. 'I don't know its name. I just heard it and liked it.'

'So you learned to play it?'

'My friend Isaac taught me to play. Back in London. And now I just hear a tune, then have a go. I don't know what that one's called.'

'If you can play it, you ought to know its name. It was written by Stephen Foster, who called it *Beautiful Dreamer*.'

'*Beautiful Dreamer*.' Vinnie nodded and remembered the dreams he and Isaac used to share.

'Your friend taught you well.' Miss Armstrong lowered herself into his chair. She indicated the bed and Vinnie sat, too; then she gave him a long, enquiring look. 'I noticed you outside my window this morning.'

'I was just listening,' Vinnie said quickly. It sounded like a confession.

'I must say, that garden bed has never been so thoroughly weeded. Flowers went too, I noticed.'

'Sorry. I don't know much about them. Flowers – weeds; weeds – flowers.'

'You find the music special, then?'

'Special.' He nodded agreement. 'Very special. It's everything.'

'Did your friend Isaac come away with you from London? Is he here, in Netterfold?'

Vinnie paused, then said slowly, 'He's not here. Because, um— because—' He struggled to hold back his tears.

'Ah.' Miss Armstrong understood. 'That first air raid, was it?'

'Yes.'

'Then one day, perhaps you'll tell me about Isaac.'

'I'll tell you now, ma'am.' Vinnie spoke in a sudden rush. 'I'll tell you now.' He hadn't talked to anyone about what had happened. Not a soul. No one had asked him, and he'd gone on since London putting an all-right face on it when it wasn't all right at all. 'Isaac,' he began, and with her eyes Miss Armstrong encouraged him, 'Isaac was a genius. He could give you any tune you wanted, playing on that old pub piano; beer and fag stains all over it. He could play one minute and make everyone laugh and sing, then next minute give you something so sad and sweet the whole pub went dead quiet. That's genius. And now it's gone. He's gone. Isaac.' Vinnie took a breath, then whispered, 'All his music, lost.'

He had more tears in his eyes, and let them fall. Miss Armstrong rested both hands on her walking stick and looked at the floor. She nodded slow agreement. 'Yes, that is a loss.'

* * *

Mrs Watney's bathroom was old-fashioned. The bath had claw feet, and heavy brass taps at one end. The only light came from a small window above the bath. There was no blackout screen on it as there was in their bedroom.

Joey protested, 'Do I have to take a bath?'

'Of course you do,' Kathleen said, 'but you can have first go at the hot water.' As she closed the door, Dennis came past on the landing. He said nothing; just glowered as he went past into his bedroom.

'There's no bolt on the door.' Joey watched the hot water running into the bath. 'We'll have to whistle *Ten Green Bottles* so people know we're in here.'

'Don't fill it too much, Joey. Mrs Watney says we can only have four inches.'

'Who takes a ruler to the bathroom?' Joey started unbuttoning his shirt.

Kathleen turned off the hot water, 'In you hop, and don't take too long.'

'You're not staying, are you?'

'No – now hurry up.' As Kathleen was about to leave the bathroom, the door suddenly swung open and Dennis stood there. He said nothing, just stood looking.

'Bathroom's occupied,' Kathleen told him.

'Didn't know anyone was in here,' Dennis muttered. 'I'll come back later.'

'And be sure to knock first,' Kathleen reminded him. 'Knock-knock, the door. From the outside.'

Dennis didn't like being spoken to like that. 'It was an accident,' he said roughly. 'Accident, plain and simple, that's what it was. Right?'

'You knew we were here,' Kathleen accused him. After the wireless rudeness, she wasn't in the mood to accept his excuse.

'Well, you're taking too long,' Dennis countered. 'I been working, see? And I need a shave.' He pointed to the window. 'It's dark soon and there's no light in here – and besides, it's me that gets the coal to heat the water. Remember that!'

'We won't be long.' Kathleen turned away to help Joey off with his shirt. Behind her back she heard the bathroom door close with a slam.

'That'll teach him,' Joey whispered.

Kathleen smiled. She had marked out a boundary.

*   *   *

At breakfast the next morning, Vinnie felt better than he'd done since leaving London. Even before he sat down at the kitchen table he was bubbling to tell Mrs Greenwood about it. 'I met Miss Armstrong last night.'

'That's nice.'

'She's all right, isn't she?' At that moment there came the sound of the gramophone playing a piano solo. Vinnie recognised it as a Jewish piece that Isaac used to play.

Mrs Greenwood put a loaf of bread and margarine on the table, then opened the connecting door to the main part of the house. The sound was clearer. 'There, that's better,' Mrs Greenwood said. 'I like to listen, too.'

For Vinnie, something clicked into place. 'All that piano music,' he asked, 'that's Miss Armstrong playing? Her own records?'

Mrs Greenwood sliced the bread. 'She used to be a musician. Famous, she was. Gave concerts all over the world; then she got arthritis. First one hand went, then the other.'

'I saw her fingers,' Vinnie said, 'all twisted and crooked. She could never play again, not with hands like that.' Vinnie listened to the music that Miss Armstrong had once played with long, strong fingers. He had told her about his sadness, and now he understood hers.

There came a click at the back door and, without knocking, a girl entered. She looked to be about four years older than Vinnie and half a head taller, with fair hair falling to her shoulders. She was fresh in the face, as if she spent a lot of time out of doors. The girl carried a basket hooked over her arm. 'Hullo, Mrs G. This is really, really peculiar.'

'Good morning, Joan,' Mrs Greenwood returned the greeting. 'Meet our house guest, Vinnie Cartwright.'

'Oh, you're one of that lot.' Joan looked Vinnie up and down, turned away, then spoke again to Mrs Greenwood: 'There's a hundred vaccies in the village. Some rough ones, like gypsies.'

Vinnie took his plate and cup to the sink. 'There's only fifteen of us,' he said. He'd already discounted Ralph DuPreis and his friend, who weren't really evacuees: they were just up from London, visiting friends in the country.

'Well, anyway Mrs G,' Joan said, 'what about this?' She took two yellow packets of custard powder from her basket. 'I found them lying outside.'

'Found them?' Puzzled, Mrs Greenwood took the packets.

'One by the back door, the other on the grass, near the flower beds.' Joan went on, 'Who'd throw away custard powder? Whole packets? Not even opened!'

'It might be poisoned,' Vinnie suggested. 'Dropped by the Germans.'

'Well, I'm not eating it,' Joan said and folded her arms.

'I'll talk with Constable Breedon.' Mrs Greenwood put the two packets on a shelf. 'Now, Vinnie, if you'd like there are some leaves to rake up.' Then she became mock stern. 'But touch not a single flower!'

He grinned. 'Miss Armstrong already chipped me about that.'

At this, Joan looked at him sharply. 'Miss Armstrong? You met her?'

Mrs Greenwood said, 'Joan, you can do the washing up here. And off with you, Vinnie. Don't go eating any German custard powder.'

'Or Jerry crystals.' Vinnie smiled and went outside to find a rake.

*   *   *

Kathleen found paper and a pencil and wrote a letter:

> *Dear Mum,*
> *We are doing well here and our billet is*
> *comfortable, the people very—*

She thought of writing 'generous', but if Mrs Watney read this private letter, she might think it was sarcastic or something. Kathleen wrote 'nice', and moved on:

> *The village is peaceful and quiet, but Joey*
> *and I worry about you in the air raids. And*
> *Joey asks if you can send his train set, and some*
> *books for me, please.*
> *The train journey here was very long and hot,*
> *but the scenery was lovely. We had music most*
> *of the way.*

It was difficult, what with wanting to tell her mother the truth, but not worry her. Kathleen bit the end of her pencil, then added:

> *Joey and I would love to hear from you,*
> *Mum, just to know you are all right and if there*
> *is any news from Daddy. We miss you both.*
> *Love from Kathleen. xxx*

*   *   *

Vinnie was in the kitchen finishing his biscuit and glass of milk. Joan opened the back door to Constable Breedon. 'Morning, Joan, morning Mrs Greenwood,' he said. 'Just want a word with your vaccy lad.' He stood red-faced and wheezing with heaviness.

'His name's Vinnie Cartwright,' Mrs Greenwood told him.

Constable Breedon nodded, then faced Vinnie. 'Packets of custard powder, lying outside the back door,' he began. 'How do you think they got there, young fella?'

'I don't know.' Vinnie folded his arms defiantly, and added, 'Sir.'

'Stealing food in wartime's a very serious offence,' the constable went on.

'Vinnie didn't leave the house last night,' Mrs Greenwood said.

'He *could* have sneaked out,' Joan put in. 'The back door's never locked.'

'Joan, Madam's lying down, so you can tidy the music room.' Mrs Greenwood nodded in that direction.

'I was only saying,' Joan muttered and huffed away.

'And don't touch Madam's piano. Whatever you do.'

Constable Breedon persisted with Vinnie: 'So, lad, you never left the house?'

'What is this? We vaccies turn up and straight off we're guilty?'

'Just answer the question,' the man said doggedly.

'You can take my dabs if you like.' Vinnie held up his hands, palms outward.

'Dabs?'

'Fingerprints,' Vinnie said. 'It's what we call them in London.'

'Ah,' Constable Breedon grunted, 'so you know all them criminal words, eh?'

Mrs Greenwood intervened. 'Constable, Vinnie said he knows nothing about the custard powder. This isn't why I rang you. He's just got here and hasn't even found his way around, so maybe you ought to look somewhere else.'

'Just letting newcomers know they should watch their step.' Constable Breedon wasn't giving up easily. 'So I'll say good morning to you, Mrs Greenwood.' With a warning frown in Vinnie's direction, Constable Breedon took a look around the kitchen, as if there might be a cup of tea on the go. There wasn't, so he left.

Mrs Greenwood shook her head. 'Never mind, Vinnie.'

*   *   *

There was no putting it off. The following Monday came around and it was time for the evacuees to enrol in Netterfold Primary School.

The bus driver, Mr Preston, still seemed unhappy with the world. He sat hunched over the steering wheel and barely looked up when Vinnie came aboard. Kathleen was already sitting alongside Joey. Dobbs was in the seat behind.

'Wotcher, Kath, wotcher Joey,' Vinnie greeted them, Cockney fashion, as he took the seat beside Dobbs and asked, 'You get a visit from the law?'

'I did.' Dobbs puffed his cheeks and stuck out his stomach. 'Scotland Yard on a bike with flat tyres. Asking about stolen food.'

'That's the man.' Vinnie laughed. 'There was some mystery custard powder found outside my billet. He accused me of nicking it.'

Joey turned around in his seat, squirming excitedly. 'Guess what, Vinnie? I can watch trains!'

Kathleen explained: 'The railway line runs along beside a street near our billet. So Joey's happy. Well, happier.' With finger and thumb, she indicated the amount.

'We've already been twice,' Joey added. 'There's a goods yard, too. Wagons everywhere.'

Mr Preston started his engine, but waited as the local boys and girls got on the bus and stalked in single file to the rear seats. As they passed, they gave the evacuees sour looks. At the back of the bus Freddie Preston called out, 'You vaccies better not be going to our school.'

'Yeah,' a local girl added nastily, 'place'll need to be funigated.'

'I think that's *fumigated*,' Kathleen remarked over her shoulder.

'Oh, my,' the girl sneered. 'Clever, are we?'

Kathleen caught Vinnie's eye and shrugged. It was not going to be nice.

few weeks ago. One of the world's most famous
men i.e. Hitler. Said that he wanted ~~he wanted~~
part Czechoslovakia. Through this fact an Inte
crisis was caused. Last week the crisis was at
to worst, I will give you my experiences durin
that ~~week~~ :—

On Monday the order came through that
families were to go to the Turnham Road S
and be fitted for Gas Masks I and my frien
Donald Broome-Smith were the first ones in ou
respective families to see this notice. So at t
first possible moment we told our Mothers a
t. On Monday Evening we all went down to
and were fitted for our Gas Masks.

On Tuesday morning Mr Green said " Owing t
the council evacuation scheme all boys who over
twenty minutes walk away from this schoo
and who are coming must bring their lu
on Wednesday morning". I as soon as ~~soon a~~
got home I told my mother about the deve
At once she packed a case full of clothes
and a satchel full of food. On Wednesd
I brought my luggage to school and put
in in the ~~classroom~~. Gradually the situ
got worse and worse. But at four o'cl

Chapter Eight
IN THE LINE OF FIRE

Netterfold Primary School was a small place in a peaceful setting, with fields of grazing sheep and cows in the background. It was beautiful outside the school grounds, but with their unfriendly attitude the locals spoiled the inside.

Vinnie, Kathleen, Dobbs and four other evacuees, two boys and two girls, were in Class Seven. Joey was in a lower class, and when the bell rang for them to go in he grabbed Kathleen's hand. She tried to cheer him up and Vinnie helped out with a promise: 'After school, we can watch trains.'

'All right.' Joey brightened and went off to his classroom.

Vinnie, Kathleen and Dobbs followed the crowds to their own classroom.

'I say, you chaps.' Dobbs put on a posh accent. 'I wonder, where is Ralphie and his chum?'

'Can't see them coming here,' Kathleen said.

'Yeah, not a cricket pitch in sight,' Vinnie added, then laughed to hide his anxiety.

The evacuees found desks on the left side of their room, under the window. Freddie Preston and five other local boys and girls sat in a group near the door, muttering among themselves. Kathleen whispered to Vinnie and Dobbs, 'We could be here for a whole year. Putting up with…with *this*.'

Vinnie nodded and got to his feet, then faced the locals. 'Listen, you lot. We didn't ask to come here. So how about you get used to it?'

At that moment, the classroom door opened and an elderly man entered. He had to be their teacher. The locals suddenly sat bolt upright, looking ahead with folded arms. The teacher stabbed a finger at Vinnie and demanded in a growl, 'What do you think you're doing, boy?'

Vinnie froze while Freddie Preston and another local boy wore sudden smiles that said 'now you're for it'. The teacher wore half-glasses that glinted coldly in the morning light. He looked at Vinnie, then repeated his question: 'I asked, what do you think you're doing? Standing there as if you're about to make a speech.'

'I was doing nothing,' Vinnie answered and sat down.

'Nothing, *sir*,' the teacher growled. 'Remember that. In this classroom, you need to know who is *sir* and who is not *sir*.'

'Yes,' Vinnie responded and added, 'sir.'

The teacher's eyes landed on a local boy who still wore a bonnet. 'And you, ill-mannered galoot, never, *never* wear a hat indoors. Not in my classroom. Do you understand?' The boy whipped his bonnet off and lowered his head.

The teacher didn't bother giving his name, but the evacuees found out later he was Mr Murdoch. He'd retired two years earlier, but since younger teachers had gone to fight the war he'd been coaxed back to the classroom.

After his abrupt introduction, Vinnie was on his guard. Mr Murdoch wasn't out to make friends, calling one local 'a great hollow lump of uselessness', another a 'wet weed'. The locals already knew him and were wary. The vaccies and the locals had a common enemy, but it didn't unite them.

On that first morning, Mr Murdoch entered the evacuee names in the roll book. It went calmly enough until it was Dobbs' turn. He stood up and said politely, but with a heavy Polish accent that he hadn't had before, 'Kind sir, I have the honour to be Dobroslaw Szczepanski.'

'Eh?' Mr Murdoch looked over the top of his glasses. 'Never mind the honour, boy. Just give me your name.'

'That is my name, kind sir. Dobroslaw Szczepanski.'

Mr Murdoch gave a heavy sigh, then started to write in the roll book, but gave up. 'So spell it. If you're able.'

Dobroslaw Szczepanski began to spell his name, letter by letter, and Mr Murdoch added them one by one to the roll book. When Dobbs finished his first name, he waved a finger to demonstrate how the 'l' should be written. He explained, 'In my country, kind sir, we put a stroke through it.'

'In this country, we don't!' Mr Murdoch retorted. 'And never mind the kind sir routine. Sir will do. Now, let's have your next name.'

Dobroslaw started spelling 'Szczepanski', but with so many jostling 'c's and 'z's, Mr Murdoch became confused. He made three attempts and ended up with a blot in the book. Eventually he growled, 'I'm still hoping for a vowel to come along soon.'

'Sir, if it makes it easier for you, my friends just call me Dobbs Stefanski.'

'Well, I'm not your friend,' Mr Murdoch snarled. 'I'm your teacher.'

'Thank you, teacher sir.' Dobbs sat down and exchanged a wink with Vinnie. Mr Murdoch closed the roll book, then opened his mouth to speak. At that moment, the school bell rang for a special morning assembly. So he contented himself with a surly frown and let the class go.

As they left the classroom, Vinnie said to Dobbs, 'You'll have to keep that phoney accent going forever.'

'Yeah – fun, ain't it?'

* * *

The special assembly was to check that every Year Five, Six and Seven student had a gas mask and knew how to fit it. Only Vinnie and two other evacuees didn't have the proper mask, so they were each promised one.

The gas-mask drill was held in the school's coal cellar, which doubled as an air-raid shelter. Teachers and students assembled dutifully on long, backless seats, wearing their masks. Some boys discovered that if they breathed out quickly, the air burst noisily from the sides of their masks where the rubber pressed against their cheeks.

Before long the cellar was filled with farting noises. This annoyed the teachers, but their voices were muffled and some of them made rude noises of their own as they tried to regain control. But students had to breathe in and out, especially out. So the noise continued.

At last the drill was over and everyone was allowed outside for morning break. In the playground, Joey ran to Kathleen, who took one look at him and asked, 'What's making you so happy?'

'My teacher's really, really nice. She's even better than the one in London.'

'Can we come to your class?' Vinnie asked.

'You're too big, and I've got to go. I'm playing marbles with my friends. One's called Jimmy and the other's Albert.'

In the playground, Freddie Preston and the locals kept to themselves. They huddled in a sulky group, muttering and sometimes glowering at the evacuees. Meanwhile, two of the local girls started skipping with a rope, chanting in time:

> *Bobby Shaftoe's gone to sea*
> *Silver buckles at his knee*
> *He'll come back to marry me*
> *Bonny Bobby Shaftoe*

They skipped on for a bit, then stopped. Something more interesting was about to happen...

As if with one mind, the locals marched towards Vinnie, Kathleen and Dobbs. 'We heard some of you got spoken to,' Freddie Preston announced, 'by Constable Breedon.'

'How'd you hear that?' Vinnie asked.

Freddie ignored this. 'We know you lot came from a slum, with dozens of criminals. So we're watching you. Got it?'

A girl pointed to Vinnie and said, 'Cowardy, cowardy custard! That's you, isn't it?'

Vinnie thought, *Custard, eh? So, word about those mysterious packets has already got around.*

With that job well done, the locals went off, still in their group. The bell rang for the end of the morning break.

Kathleen spoke gloomily: 'So this is to be our school? Nasty outside, and nasty in?'

'Yeah, out here's the frying pan, in there's the

fire.' Vinnie pointed to the classrooms. Kathleen managed a smile.

* * *

When class resumed, Mr Murdoch took a piece of chalk and started writing a row of numbers at the top of the blackboard. Below this, he added more numbers until the blackboard looked like this:

```
1 2 4 6 8 9 0 4 7 3 8 0 9 1 2 0 8 9 8 4 8 7 6 9
              1 5 4 8 9 3 5 2 9 0 3 5 1 2 8 0
    4 6 7 8 9 3 4 5 6 1 2 9 5 6 8 4 5 6 2 4 8 9 7 6
              7 8 4 8 5 6 2 9 0 2 7 8 9 0 1 3
9 3 9 4 8 5 7 6 1 9 2 1 7 8 9 4 5 6 2 7 8 4 5 6 0
              3 5 7 2 8 1 9 0 3 5 6 3 7 8 0
3 5 6 7 8 9 2 3 4 9 7 6 8 2 3 4 5 6 7 8 3 4 5 9 0
              8 7 5 6 7 6 4 3 5 2 4 5 7 6 7
```

And still he wrote on! It took him a full five minutes of silent concentration until he had written nine rows of figures. He finished with a plus sign then drew a long line under the numbers. In his menacing voice, he said, 'Just do that sum. See if you can get it right for once.' Then he went to his desk, took out a newspaper and began to read.

In silence the class opened their exercise books, copied the numbers and then started to add them up. It was all they did for the rest of the morning, just that one huge sum.

About five minutes before the bell rang to signal

the lunch recess, Mr Murdoch took an aloof interest. He asked only the local boys and girls to give their answers to the sum. Only two of them got the same number. Vinnie noticed that they sat next to each other, so maybe that had helped.

Mr Murdoch said, 'Well, that seems to be the answer.' Then the bell rang and without another word he walked out. The locals followed; then the evacuees went chattering from the room.

In the afternoon, it was silent reading, but few of the evacuees had books. The locals, who knew about this sort of lesson, eagerly produced library books and settled down. Vinnie noticed that Freddie Preston had a large book propped up on his desk with a *Dandy* comic hidden inside. Mr Murdoch wasn't the kind of teacher to pace between the rows of desks, so Freddie was quite safe reading his comic.

As for the evacuees, the only books most of them had were the arithmetic and English grammar texts already in their desks. The afternoon passed slowly. At last the bell sounded.

And the final mean lesson of the afternoon: Freddie Preston and his mates made a rapid beeline for the school bus, which took off for Netterfold leaving everyone else behind. 'Well,' Vinnie said, 'we're learning. We won't get caught like that again.'

'It's as if we've left one war,' Kathleen observed, 'only to come to another.'

It was a long trudge back to the village, but Vinnie

had his harmonica, so he cheered them on by playing 'The Grand Old Duke of York' and other marching tunes. When he got tired of it, the evacuees whistled 'Colonel Bogey' until Dobbs made them giggle by marching a gigantic goosestep with his long legs. Then the ground began to shake.

They faced each other, puzzled. Joey moved closer to Kathleen. Next came the noise – a dull roar. Alarmed, they looked to the sky, but it was not coming from there.

Dobbs pointed. 'It's not a Gerry, it's ours!' Around a bend in the road they'd just walked came an army tank so wide it almost brushed the hedgerows on each side. A commander stood high in the turret, his beret at an angle.

Vinnie, Kathleen, Joey and Dobbs scrambled up on a farm gate as the tank surged nearer. The commander held up two hands with all fingers outstretched and nodded behind him, then roared on his way.

'He means ten more to come,' Vinnie said. They sat on their gate and watched as tank after tank growled past, each one with a friendly commander in the turret, who'd give them a wave, a wink or a thumbs-up.

'What about the size of them!' Vinnie was amazed.

Dobbs held his hands apart. 'The tracks are that wide.'

'We should have a flag,' Joey said. 'To show we're on their side.'

When the last tank had roared away, the evacuees

resumed walking back to their billets. At a T-junction in the road they could see from the marks on the ground that the tanks had swung left and not gone through the village.

'If we'd got the bus, we'd never have seen them,' Kathleen remarked.

* * *

In the village, they found Freddie Preston and his friends outside the post office, arms folded, leaning against a wall. The locals were slyly amused at the success of their stunt with the school bus.

Dobbs said, 'I'll just have a word with Friendly Freddie.'

'You mean the enemy.' Kathleen shook her head to warn Dobbs to let it go.

'Only a *little* word,' he assured her with a dangerous wink, then approached the locals. 'Wotcher, Fred! What about that stupid bus driver, leaving us vaccies behind?'

Freddie bridled. 'That stupid bus driver's my brother, George.'

Dobbs shook his head in a sympathetic way. 'So, George is your stupid brother, eh?'

Freddie realised his mistake. He ground his teeth. 'Just watch it, you.'

'Tell me,' Dobbs persisted. 'Why isn't George in uniform?'

Freddie sprang upright. 'What do you mean?' He raised a fist. 'What do you mean by that?'

'Bus driver's uniform,' Dobbs explained. 'Don't they have them here? We've got them in London. Tram drivers, too. They're all in uniform. With a badge. And a cap.'

Having done enough damage, he smiled and pushed past Freddie into the post office. The door went *ding*, like the bell you get at a boxing match.

'End of round one,' Vinnie said loudly, so that Freddie could hear.

'And I think Dobbs won it,' Kathleen added. Freddie scowled, dropped his eyes and looked away.

Joey said, 'Vinnie, do you still want to see the railway? There might be a train coming.'

'All right, one train, Joey,' Vinnie agreed and sang a line from a wartime song: '*Then it's back to our billets we crawl.*'

'*Bless 'em all,*' Kathleen added, and when she got back to her billet, there was a letter waiting for her.

NO TIME

MR WHITE: Who were you talking to at the door? he kept you standing there for ver half an hour.

Mrs White: It was only Irs Black calling to leave a essage for us. She said she adn't time to come in.

Indian Proverbs

We hasty are deficient in sense.

Train a boy strictly, a girl kindly.

Whom will he help that does not help his mother?

Quietness is worth much gold.

he coward blames his weapon.

Other Worlds Next Week

N the evening the planet Mercury is in the south-west, Jupiter

and Saturn are close together in the south, and Uranus is in the south-east. In the morning Venus is low in the south-east

id Mars is in the south. The icture shows the Moon as it may e seen at 8 o'clock on Sunday orning, February 16.

Hidden Birds

N each of the following sentences is concealed the name of a well-nown bird.

Nobody could be expected to ook anything well in this old oven. That boy will certainly grow like s father.

The drummers and pipers were aying an inspiring march.

Gerald helped the fishermen haul nets full of fish.

We are going to buy a house now; ts are too expensive.

If you can stay to tea, let me now as soon as possible.

Answer next week

How Captain Cook Wrote His Name

APTAIN JAMES COOK, a Yorkshire-man, is one of the finest figures English naval history, for he ecame the greatest explorer of the acific by sheer world. The son of farm labourer, he entered the avy as a seaman; but only four ears later he was commanding a ip. His name will always be sociated with New Zealand, the oast of which he explored, while also helped to build the world bout Australia. He was killed by vages in Hawaii on February 14, 779, when little more than fifty. his is how he wrote his name:

Jas† Cook

THE PUBLISHER POLITE

A Japanese publishing house announced its books in this way:

READERS will find the under-mentioned advantages at our house of business:

1. The price is cheap as in a lottery.

2. The printing as clear as crystal.

3. The books as elegant as an opera singer.

4 The paper as strong as the hide of an elephant.

5. The books forwarded as quick as the shot of a gun.

6. Parcels treated with as much care as that expended by a loving wife on her husband.

A Painful Ending

YOU never hear the bee complain, Or hear it weep or wail; But if it wish it can unfold A very painful tail.

What A Tear is Made of

AN analysis of a human tear shows that it contains 984 parts of water and almost sixteen parts of salt. In addition there are tiny traces of albuminoids, organic matter, and sulphates and phosphates. As far as can be discovered, tears do not vary whatever the cause of their coming may be.

Jacko Adds to the Fun

BIG SISTER BELINDA, her mother used to say, had a beautiful singing voice. Neddy, with a little gentle persuasion from Jacko, admired it so much that he joined in the concert. You never heard such a noise!

Ici on Parle Français

A Robin in a Pit

An engine-driver working at the bottom of a colliery shaft was surprised to see a little robin hopping merrily along in the darkness. He picked it up, and put it into a jar with a supply of food and water.

The robin had been caught in the current of air drawn to the pit, which is 1800 feet deep.

After the day's work was over the engine-driver ascended the pit, taking the robin with him. Then the little bird was released, and flew up into the air, quite happy and none the worse for its adventure.

Un Rouge-gorge dans une Mine

Un mécanicien, travaillant au fond du puits d'une mine, fut surpris de voir un petit rouge-gorge sautillant gaîment dans l'obscurité. Il le ramassa et le mit dans une cruche avec de quoi manger et boire.

Le rouge-gorge avait été emporté par le courant d'air amené à la mine, qui a 1800 pieds de profondeur.

Sa journée finie, le mécanicien remonta à la surface, emportant le rouge-gorge. Puis, le petit oiseau fut remis en liberté et s'envola parfaitement heureux, n'ayant pas souffert de son aventure.

THE UP-TO-DATE MOLE

SAID a clever and businesslike mole:

"I will burrow until I strike coal: Then my mining rights I Will persuade folks to buy, And in riches thenceforward I'll roll!"

A Diphphiculty Overcome

One day there was a mishap in the office of a local paper, and the next number contained this notice:

THE proprietors ov the Phree Press regret to inphorm their phaithphul readers that the curious appearance ov this issue is due to an unphortunate accident in our printing department. One ov our assistants had a mishap with our letter ephs, all ov which were destroyed. We phound that it was too late phor us to obtain a phresh supply in time phor this issue, so we were therephore phorced to phall back on "ph" and "v," which may be epliphective but not beautiphul.

No doubt our phriends will phorgive our shortcomings this week when we assure them that we shall not phail to appear in our usual phorm in phuture.

A MONEY PROBLE

A MAN had thirty-five sh made up of five half-cr four florins, and twent sixpences, and he decid divide the sum equally be his two sons.

He found that he could each of them the same a and the same number of c

What coins did the receive?

Answer n

Separating the Prisoners

IN a certain European c twenty men were impr in a fortress, the cells of whi represented by this drawing.

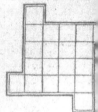

were four English, four F four German, four Russian four Italian prisoners.

They were so placed that of them had one of his own co men in an adjoining cell. Ho this done?

Answer n

Do You Live in Coventry?

THIS name has nothing to do a convent, but was origi spelt Cofantreo, which is English for the tree by the co chamber.

No doubt in the early day site of this city was marke some tall or outstanding tre grew near a cave, and when a ment of people occurred the place was called after the tre

A Great Idea

A WELL-KNOWN scientist had a lecture in which he tioned that many of the mo portant scientific discoveries result of pure accident.

As he left the lecture ha scientist met a lady who tol that she quite believed wh had said because she had made a great discovery herse

"Indeed, madam, I shoul to hear about it." he said.

"Well," said the lady, "covered, quite accidentally, t you keep an ink-pot handy yo use a fountain-pen just as as an ordinary one, and, w more, you don't have the me trouble of filling it."

C N STRIP

FIVE KINDS OF BRIDGE

Chapter Nine
LESSONS OF A DIFFERENT KIND

From London, Susannah Pearson wrote to her children in Netterfold:

My darling Kathleen and Joey,

I've been so worried about you, but your letters cheered me up. You must write to tell me everything, and I do mean every *little thing.*

I'm afraid there is a problem about sending Joey's train set and your books, Kathleen. There was another air raid last night, and our house received some damage. The ARP people won't allow me inside until it is safe.

As you can see from my new address, I'm living somewhere else for the time being.

I know you love reading your Dandy *or* Beano, *Joey dear, so I'm enclosing a postal order for you both to spend. Maybe you can buy a book, Kathleen.*

That's all for now, darlings. Daddy's well; I had a letter from him from Galveston, in Texas. His ship is a new oil tanker. Very fast, he says, and sends his love, as I do.

Keep safe for your loving mother. xxxx

Kathleen read the letter; when Joey came back from watching trains, he read it for himself.

'It's good that Mum and Dad are safe,' he said, then, 'Where's our postal order, Kathleen?'

Instead of answering, she teased him: 'It's somewhere secret. I'll pop along to the post office and cash it.'

Joey persisted. 'How much money did Mum send?'

'Just you wait and see.' Kathleen bit her lip and turned away. Their mother's letter had been opened and the postal order removed. She'd kept this from Joey. It was one thing to leave their letters open to let Mrs Watney 'add her own note', as she'd said. It was something else for Mrs Watney to open letters that Kathleen and Joey *received*.

Kathleen hated the idea of questioning a grown-up. She put a bright face on. 'How were the trains, Joey?'

'Big and black,' he answered. 'Like Dennis when he comes home after being out at night.'

* * *

Miss Armstrong's room was comfortable, and the air was filled with soaring piano music coming from a large gramophone. It was an electric gramophone in a polished wooden cabinet, not the wind-up-with-a-handle kind that Vinnie knew. 'Come in, Vinnie,' Miss Armstrong greeted him.

'Mrs Greenwood said you wanted to see me, ma'am.' But he wondered, *Why has she sent for me? Is it about that business with the custard powder? This place is so good, I don't want to leave. And go where?* The worry showed on his face.

Miss Armstrong faded the music, then turned off the gramophone and said, 'Vinnie, I enjoyed your playing the other day. *Beautiful Dreamer.*'

He was relieved. 'Thank you, ma'am.'

'I have to confess, I paused for quite a while, listening at your bedroom door.'

'I didn't know that.' Vinnie wondered how long she'd been out there.

'Your friend Isaac taught you? Yes?'

'Not the harmonica. I learned to play that myself. Isaac taught me the piano.'

Miss Armstrong seemed impressed. 'And you read music, too?'

'Not really, ma'am. I just pick out tunes. Hear them, then have a go.'

This amused Miss Armstrong. She pointed to a corner of the room. 'Would you like to *have a go* on my piano?'

Vinnie looked. This piano was entirely different

from the one in the pub: it was huge and so highly polished it almost glowed with its dark beauty. 'Is that a *grand* piano?' He was in awe.

'It is indeed. And you're going to have a go on it.'

Vinnie discovered how to lift the lid then carefully prop it open at an angle. Inside he could see the strings and the hammers, so many of them. He sat at Miss Armstrong's grand piano and faced the keys, which seemed to go on forever to the left and the right. Vinnie read the name in front of the keyboard: Steinway. 'Isaac had a Broadwood,' he said. 'He told me. In his house, in Germany.'

'Some Nazi has it now.'

Miss Armstrong nodded. 'Beethoven owned a Broadwood. He hammered so loudly on the keys he almost destroyed it. Poor man had gone quite deaf.' She paused. 'Terrible for a musician to be so afflicted.'

'I've heard about Beethoven,' he told her. Then, as if the Steinway had invited him, he played a chord. The invasion of sound took him by surprise. Vinnie smiled, then looked at Miss Armstrong. 'Isaac would love this.'

'Then you can love it too, so play something for me.'

Vinnie thought. It couldn't be a pub tune, some knees-up rumpy-tump piece, not on a piano so imposing. He remembered a sweet French song that Isaac had been fond of, so he played it through.

When he finished, Vinnie was regretful, because he never wanted to stop the sounds that came from this piano.

'Bravo! Vinnie, how lovely to hear my Tessie ring out again.'

'Tessie?'

'My piano. When the delivery men first brought her in, one of them said, *Missus, that's like shifting Two Ton Tessie O'Shea*. So that's what I call her.' She was amused by the story. 'So thank you, Vinnie, for your music, and the memory.'

'No, thank you, for letting me play. And thanks… Tessie.' He put his hand gently on the piano.

'You're going to come again?' Then without waiting, she went on, 'Of course you will; you can't let your ability wither away.' Miss Armstrong brought her hands together, then lifted them and kissed her thumbs. She became brisk. 'Vinnie, you must learn to read music properly. There is so much for you to know. But are you eager enough?'

'I'm eager.' He sat nodding at the keyboard until Tessie encouraged him to play again. This time it was 'Beautiful Dreamer'.

* * *

Mrs Watney was in the kitchen, scrubbing a saucepan with wire wool. Kathleen steeled herself, then began: 'Mrs Watney, we had a letter from our mother.'

'So I saw,' Mrs Watney replied, and scrubbed on.

'Mum mentioned a postal order.' Kathleen stopped

herself from asking if Mrs Watney had taken the postal order. She waited.

Mrs Watney put the saucepan down and wiped her hands. She was still not satisfied with how clean it was, so gave the surface another wipe, then said without looking up: 'I was going to cash it for you. Give you the money.'

At that moment Dennis came in, walking on his heels, carrying lumps of coal in a dusty sack. 'It's heavy, Mum. Make way for the coal man. Special delivery.'

Mrs Watney rushed to assist him. 'Oh, Dennis, shoot it into the coal box, darling.'

Kathleen kept calm and waited while Dennis rumbled the coal into a brass box that stood beside the kitchen stove. Dust rose. Kathleen tried again. 'There's no need for you to bother, Mrs Watney. I know where the post office is.'

Mrs Watney seemed to be totally absorbed in the coal, opening the door on the stove and adding a couple of lumps to the fire.

Dennis said, 'That'll keep us going, eh, Mum?' He looked sharply at Kathleen and added, 'Keeps the bath water hot as well.'

After a pause, Kathleen persisted: 'So, Mrs Watney, if I could have it. Please.'

Mrs Watney took the postal order from her apron pocket and put it on the kitchen table. Kathleen had to reach over for it and found a dark coal smudge on one corner. She seethed with anger, but decided to leave it at this, ignoring the business of her mother's personal letter being read. That was a battle to be fought later.

*　*　*

Next morning, before boarding the school bus, Kathleen and Joey went into the post office. Mrs Hall greeted them cheerfully. 'How are you settling in, my dears?' She paused, then added in another voice: 'With Mrs Watney?'

'Quite well, thank you,' Kathleen said.

Mrs Hall counted out the value of the postal order. 'Seven shillings and sixpence. My word, you two are in the money.'

Since she was so friendly, Kathleen went on, 'Um, can our mother's letters be sent here?'

'Of course they can, dear. Have your mother write on the envelope, *Post Office, Netterfold. Please hold.*'

'Then we come in to collect them?' Joey asked.

'Just like that,' Mrs Hall said. 'Why not buy a tuppenny lettercard to tell your mum right now?'

With some of the postal order money, Kathleen bought a few lettercards, then sent the new address to her mother. She wondered if her mum would understand why they were doing it.

When the lettercard was safely inside the pillar box, Joey said, 'No more snooping from the Witch of Watney.'

Dobbs joined them from the back of the shop and they went off to the bus stop. Kathleen felt she'd won a battle.

* * *

Dobbs had also won. Mr Preston now wore a peaked cap with a shiny metal badge on it saying 'BUS DRIVER'. The evacuees took their seats, staying well away from the locals. The journey to school passed peacefully enough, and when Dobbs got off he said to Mr Preston, 'We'll want the bus after school, so don't forget us, driver.'

Mr Preston spoke without looking at Dobbs. 'Yeah, just make sure you hurry up.'

And that seemed to be the end of it – not that there was any change in the locals' attitude, or in the bus driver's cheerless mood.

* * *

Mr Murdoch, deep in thought, paced the classroom floor. He looked at the ceiling, but not at the students, then asked in an ominous voice, 'What is a dictionary?'

Vinnie well knew what it was, but suspected a trick question. The local boys and girls were also wary. No one raised a hand. Mr Murdoch glowered and persisted, 'Well?' Still no one moved. 'It's a simple enough question,' he declared. 'I'll repeat it in case you've become hard of hearing.' He spaced out the words: 'What – is – a – dictionary?'

Around the room, hands went up, but none eagerly. Mr Murdoch pointed to Tom Bradley, one of the local boys, who stood and started to say, 'Sir, it's a list of words in alphabetical order—'

'No, sit down!' Mr Murdoch's impatience grew. 'Anyone else?'

Vinnie was puzzled. Tom's was the answer he'd have given. Raised hands went down. Mr Murdoch nodded to Irene, a local girl, who said, 'You get meanings from it, sir.'

'Sit down!'

Another local boy tried. 'Sir, it's got all the words in the English lan—'

'Rubbish!' Mr Murdoch favoured the locals and ignored the evacuees.

Eventually Jessie, another local girl, said, 'Sir, it's a book.'

'Correct! That's what it is. It's a *book*.'

Kathleen looked at Dobbs, then at Vinnie, who shrugged. The gesture didn't escape the teacher's attention. He stormed to the evacuee side of the room to demand, 'Do you London fellas have something clever to say?'

'No, sir. We are not clever people,' Dobbs said in his Polish accent. 'The Germans took over my country in only twenty-six days. So we are not clever.'

Mr Murdoch paused, then said, 'Well, pay attention. You might learn something.' He prowled to the local side of the classroom to ask, 'What *kind* of a book is it?'

Irene answered, 'Sir, it's an English book.'

'Yes, yes! At last. It's an *English* book. The dictionary is an English book.'

Dobbs raised his hand. The teacher turned back

to the locals. Dobbs called out in his accent, 'Sir, if it was a *Polish* dictionary, then it would not be an English book.'

Mr Murdoch spun around and yelled, 'How dare you speak without being told?'

'But it's true, sir, is it not?' Dobbs insisted. 'We haff dictionaries in Poland that are not English dictionaries.'

Vinnie joined in: 'And what if it's a Dutch dictionary?'

Kathleen felt the boys needed support. 'Or a French one?'

'Shut up, all of you!' Mr Murdoch bellowed.

Then it happened. Tom Bradley also spoke without leave. 'Scottish. That would not be an English book.' The other locals nodded. Some put up their hands, ready to provide the names of other countries that had non-English dictionaries.

Mr Murdoch swelled in size. He took from his desk a leather belt as long as his forearm. Dobbs had started this, and Tom Bradley had aided and abetted him. 'Out here, you two. Put your hands up!'

The belt swished savagely three times on Tom's open palm. Everyone winced. Dobbs then held his hand out. He was so tall that it was almost level with Mr Murdoch's head. He realised it was too high and asked, 'Shall I kneel down, kind sir?'

The class couldn't help itself: almost everybody burst out laughing. Vinnie thought, *Dobbs is out there, copping it. Tom Bradley, too, and for what?*

For being right. He had to join in; there was nothing else for it. He stood and asked the class, 'Hands up who knows what a dictionary is.'

Kathleen raised her hand, followed by Dobbs.

'Enough of that, enough of that!' Mr Murdoch made for Vinnie, but local hands went up. Then two evacuee girls raised their desk lids and banged them down loudly. Mr Murdoch tried to assert his authority, but he had lost control. *'Shut up! You'll all be punished! I'll belt every one of you!'*

The slamming desk lids grew louder. Two locals joined in. Then the rest.

Moments later, the headmaster burst through the door. The noise stopped. 'Mr Murdoch,' the headmaster said, 'may I have a word with you outside?'

'Um, yes, Mr Boyce.' Mr Murdoch tossed the belt on his desk and, in a distracted way, left the classroom, closing the door behind him.

Dobbs said across the room to Tom, 'Sorry you got the belt, when I started it.'

Tom grinned. 'It was worth it.'

Later in the playground, when Jessie and Irene spun the rope and skipped to 'Bobby Shaftoe', it was Irene who broke off to ask Kathleen to join in. Kathleen said yes, but she only held the end of the rope. She'd never been a good jumper. Couldn't get the timing right.

MECCANO

This splendid model of a Pontoon Crane is built entirely of standard Meccano parts.

The World's Greatest Toys

We regret that we cannot supply these famous toys to-day, but they will be ready for you again after the war. Look out for the good times coming.

HORNBY TRAINS

A Hornby Passenger Set passing under a Gantry Signal.

CCANO LIMITED, BINNS ROAD, LIVERPOOL 13

Chapter Ten
THE UNKIND TRICK

It was late November, almost three months since the evacuees had arrived in Netterfold. The weather had grown colder and darkness came early. After finishing school, Joey often wandered down to the railway yard and stood by the fence. It was good coming here; the best place in Netterfold because there was usually something interesting going on. There was a big shed where the goods wagons were pushed inside to be unloaded; then the same locomotive pulled the empty ones out again. The railway yard was always busy, with wagons coming off one track and being shunted into another one.

He'd asked Vinnie to come with him to watch

the trains today, but as usual, Vinnie had said, 'I have my piano lessons in the afternoon. Can't miss that.'

Dobbs had been the same: 'Sorry, Joey. That's when I help Mrs Hall and Henry sort the letters and parcels.'

Kathleen, too, had shaken her head. 'I've seen enough trains to last the rest of my life. But you go by yourself.'

Some of the railway men on the other side of the fence were friendly and often gave him a wave. One driver of a tank locomotive always passed by holding up his fingers in a 'V for victory' sign. He did it today, then gave a cheery blast on his whistle, as usual. It went, *Toot-toot-toot-TOOOT*, three shorts and one long, which everyone knew was •••—, morse code for 'V'. Joey waved back and the locomotive puffed on, dragging its empty goods vans behind.

When the train had passed by, a shunter stepped across the railway lines towards the fence. The man carried a long wooden pole with a hook on the end. Joey knew the shunters used the pole to couple the vans together to make a train. This shunter was Dennis Watney.

This wasn't so good. Dennis was unfriendly. Joey called him Dennis the Demon. Kathleen had a different name for him every day, Dreadful Dennis being the one she'd made up that morning.

Dennis reached the fence. 'Hullo, young Joey.'

'Yes, hello.' Joey started to move away. The fun was over.

'Looking at the engines, eh?'

'Yes.'

'The one that just went by was an 0-6-0.'

'I know that. And that one over there is a 2-6-2.' Nearly every boy in Britain knew about locomotive wheel arrangements. The famous Flying Scotsman was a 4-6-2.

Dennis leaned on his shunting pole. 'Did you hear that row last night? Outside our place?'

'I heard some shouting. In the street.'

'Big fuss over nothing.' Dennis looked up and down the railway lines. 'You got a train set, young Joey?'

'At home in London. Not here.'

'I got one. Don't use it anymore. It's in a cupboard.'

Joey became interested. 'Electric or clockwork?'

'Clockwork.' Dennis made a winding-up motion with his hand. 'It's a beauty. Tell you what, you can have a play with it, if you like.'

'Can I?'

From the goods shed, another railway man came out and shouted, 'Hey, Watney. Over here!'

Dennis said quickly, 'I've got to go, Joey. Talk later, eh?'

'All right.' Joey moved off. A train set. That would be something.

* * *

In his bedroom at night, Vinnie started talking to Isaac, in his head. It wasn't like how it had been before that awful Saturday – lying in their beds upstairs at the pub, Isaac had used to keep up his end of the conversation, but now Vinnie was alone and all he had were thoughts.

But that's not a problem, Isaac. There's plenty to say, because guess what? I'm having more piano lessons – been at it nearly three months. Can you imagine it? Me, a grubby street kid out of the East End, learning on Lila Armstrong's amazing Steinway grand piano? These are proper lessons, Isaac, and that's not to say what you taught me wasn't good, great even, but I'm doing scales and exercises now.

When it comes to practice, I do what we did on the old pub piano, before Hitler blew it away. Miss Armstrong even gave me an alarm clock so I can get up at five and put in a couple of hours before school. The house is quiet then, apart from me and that amazing piano. It makes you want to be good; not to let it down.

There's theory, too, and reading music, learning the time-value of notes – crotchets and quavers, breves and semibreves. It was funny this afternoon when I called one note a minimum instead of a minim. First time I saw her laugh. She said, 'Get it right, or I shall call you Vinnimum.'

Right now things are nice for me. But remember how we'd talk about life being full of ups and downs – good things turning bad? You think you're in clover, then you're not. Like some unkind trick. You learned music, Isaac; then the Nazis brought you down. When we found Mr and Mrs Rosen, we were up again, until that Saturday.

When it's good for me, Isaac, I get afraid of what might come.

Then he slept.

* * *

Vinnie was discovering that music had a language of its own. In the kitchen, he tried out some Italian musical terms on Mrs Greenwood as they washed the breakfast dishes. '*Fortissimo, rallentando!*' He loved making grand gestures and rolling the words around his tongue. '*Prestissimo, affettuoso, spiritoso.*'

Mrs Greenwood gave him a playful flick with her tea towel. 'Your head's just bulging with knowledge.'

'Yeah, great, isn't it?'

At this cheerful moment, Joan entered the kitchen. Mrs Greenwood glanced at the wall clock and said, 'So, *there* you are, then? What kept you this morning?'

'Me and George Preston went to the pictures over in Duffton, last night. Saw *Gone with the Wind*. Missed the bus home, had to walk miles.'

Mrs Greenwood accepted this and gave Joan the tea towel. 'Well, finish here, then tidy the music room.' With that, she left the kitchen.

Joan reached for a plate and asked Vinnie, 'So what was that language you were jabbering?'

'Only some Italian words.' He put the last of the knives and forks into the draining basket and let the water out of the sink.

'Eyeties are our enemy. Why talk their lingo? You on their side or something?'

'Musicians have used Italian words for hundreds of years. So we're not changing because there's a war going on. That's what Miss Armstrong says.'

'Oh, Miss Armstrong, everything's Miss Armstrong these days!' Joan put a plate on the rack and grabbed another one. 'You get to play her piano, while I'm not even allowed to polish it. I'd like free music lessons, but you come here and worm your way right in.'

'Yeah. Now I gotta worm off to school.'

As he walked to the bus, he thought, *Isaac, it's a funny old place, this. Full of cold hurts and hot insults. Some of the locals are friendlier now, but Freddie and one or two others still keep their distance. Mr Murdoch rules the classroom like some kind of dictator, and Joan makes the kitchen frosty, even when Mrs Greenwood's there to keep her in check. Constable Breedon is forever asking custard powder questions and nobody has an answer, but do you think that stops him?*

And Dobbs reckons our bus driver plays for Misery United.

Yet whenever I turn to music, all the slights

are soothed away. It's amazing, Isaac, that we can always find an Italian word to match our mood. Or their mood.

Furioso. Feroce.

* * *

Joey and Kathleen took their seats on the bus. 'Kathleen, what was that shouting the other night? It woke me up.'

'Somebody showed a light. Mrs Watney or Dennis didn't put up the blackout screens. Serves them right.'

'What difference does it make? The Germans aren't going to bomb Netterfold.'

Kathleen was patient. 'They might. We can't take the risk.'

'So that's what the shouting was about?'

'The ARP warden saw the light shining from a window and ordered Mrs Watney to put it out.'

Mr Preston started his engine and prepared to move off, but Tom Bradley called from the back seat, 'Hey, wait. Two more boys are coming.'

Dobbs and Vinnie climbed aboard, panting after running for the bus. Dobbs said, 'Nearly went without us, driver. That wouldn't do.'

The driver just grunted and started off with a lurch. Kathleen turned around to Vinnie and whispered, 'Tom got him to stop for you.'

Dobbs and Vinnie turned around, caught Tom's eye and both gave him a thumbs-up.

In class, the first lesson was arithmetic, the examples coming from a textbook. With his pupils quiet and busy, Mr Murdoch spent the time reading the newspaper.

Freddie Preston kept his hands under the desk, working on a secret weapon. He folded a slip of paper, then doubled it twice to make a tight wad. Using his ruler as a catapult, he fired the paper across the room towards Dobbs. It missed, but hit the wall and bounced.

Mr Murdoch chose that moment to turn a page of his newspaper and saw Freddie's attack. 'Caught in the act, boy! So come out here. And bring your exercise book.'

'It was an accident, sir.'

Mr Murdoch looked at Freddie's blank page. 'You've not done very much, have you, boy?'

'I was just starting, sir.'

'Starting a war. So hold your hand up, lad.'

Freddie rolled his eyes helplessly and lifted his hand. Mr Murdoch opened his desk, and frowned. He tossed things aside and searched more urgently. His mystification grew; then he closed the desk lid and made for the door. 'Keep working,' he warned. 'And no noise.' He left the room.

'What's he lost?' Kathleen whispered.

Vinnie said, 'Not his sense of humour. Never had one.'

Dobbs guessed, 'Bet it was his belt.'

Freddie Preston stood with his hand up, still waiting for the punishment that was not going to come. 'One of you vaccies nicked it.'

Tom Bradley called, 'Belt up, Freddie.' Some girls laughed.

Freddie went on, 'You vaccies are up to your thieving tricks. Like last night.'

Vinnie asked Dobbs, 'What about last night?'

'There was another break-in at the railway goods yard. More food went missing.'

Freddie muttered, 'Constable Breedon will fix you lot.'

Dobbs pretended to quiver with fear. 'Oo-er, he'd have us all in custard-y.'

Mr Murdoch returned. He took a hopeful look inside his desk, as if expecting to find whatever he'd lost. Then he realised Freddie still had his hand out, palm upwards, and asked, 'Are you expecting rain, boy?'

The class laughed as Freddie slouched back to his seat. Mr Murdoch saw something funny in his own joke, so he turned away to hide a smile.

* * *

At teatime, Mrs Watney said casually to Kathleen, 'I have to go to court. About the blackout thing.'

Then Dennis dropped a bombshell. 'And young Joey's got to come, too,' he said. 'To tell the magistrate what happened.'

'Joey?' Kathleen asked. 'What have you got to do with it?'

Joey looked embarrassed and kept his eyes down on his plate.

Dennis encouraged Joey. 'Go on, Joey, tell Kathleen what you did.'

Joey mumbled, 'I went into Dennis's room to get my comic—'

'I'd borrowed it from him, see.' Dennis took up the story. 'So Joey pops in to fetch it, turns the light on, only he forgets about the blackout. Gets dark and the light's still shining from my window.'

'That's what happened.' Joey nodded, then looked down again.

Kathleen said, 'You didn't tell me this, Joey.'

Joey was silent.

'Anyway,' Mrs Watney went on, 'since it was Joey's fault, really, and him not knowing any better, the magistrate will go easy on us because he's such a little chap.'

'Yeah, it's not *Joey* that's in trouble,' Dennis assured Kathleen, 'it's Mum who cops it because she's responsible for the whole house, and the blackout.'

'Does Joey have to go to court?' Kathleen asked.

'Only as a witness,' Mrs Watney said. 'Only as a witness.'

'When?'

'On Friday morning. Court's at ten o'clock, so when it's over, I'll take him to school.'

'You won't,' Kathleen said. 'I'll do that.' She was angry, with Joey for not speaking up and with the Watneys for not telling her what had happened. She tried to catch Joey's eye, but he kept his head down.

The EVER RISING TIDE

WAR production is rising like the tide, and the need for rail transport rises with it. But this increase in traffic is only *one* of the Railways' many war-time loads.

The gigantic task of dispersing to all parts of the country, men and materials from overseas falls on the Railways and they too, must fit into the running schedules the 7,000 special workers' trains run each week as they have fitted in the 150,000 special trains for military personnel and equipment since the beginning of the war.

Such is the task of British Railways, day in day out, the 24 hours round.

BRITISH RAILWAYS
GWR · LMS   LNER · SR

Carrying the War Load

Chapter Eleven
COURTING TROUBLE

The music lesson was over by five o'clock. It was the fortieth one they'd had together in the music room. Vinnie kept the tally in a small diary: three times a week they had met, except once when Miss Armstrong had the flu; then it was only one lesson, but she'd insisted he spend the rest of the time on scales and arpeggios. Vinnie closed the Steinway's keyboard cover, then lowered the prop and gently let down the main piano lid. He gathered his sheet music from the stool and waited for Miss Armstrong's remarks. At the end of a lesson she always had some advice to give.

This time she said, 'You are doing extremely well, Vinnie.'

'Thank you.'

'You know if you were showing no aptitude, or application, I'd have ended these lessons weeks ago.'

'I guessed that's why I'm still coming here.'

'Did you now?' She was amused. 'I'm going to listen to Dame Myra Hess tonight, Vinnie.'

'On one of your records?'

'No, on the wireless, from the BBC. She's playing Beethoven. Would you like to listen with me after tea?'

'Yes, I'd like that.'

'The concert will go on quite late, so you needn't stay for all of it.'

'I don't mind.'

'Then in the morning you'll want to sleep in and won't do your two hours before school.'

'I'd never miss that,' he said. And later in the evening Vinnie returned to Miss Armstrong's music room and they listened to Beethoven until the end of the broadcast. They had cocoa, then heard the news.

'Here is the BBC news and this is Alvar Lidell reading it. Tonight, enemy bombers carried out another heavy raid on London, causing wide-spread damage.'

'Vinnie, you can turn it off,' Miss Armstrong said. 'Such contrasts from Germany. In one night, Beethoven and bombs.'

He went to bed. *The good, then the bad, Isaac. Please let the right one last.*

* * *

The classroom mystery continued: what had Mr Murdoch lost? Most students guessed it was his punishing leather strap, which Vinnie and Dobbs called his Weapon of War. The main clue was that no one had been belted for over a week. Their teacher would fly into a rage, then shout, 'Out here, boy!' At the front of the class, the offender would hold up his hand, but no punishment came. Instead, Mr Murdoch would insult the boy, say he was hopeless, a dolt, a fool, then order: 'Get out of my sight!'

Dobbs came to school on Thursday morning bubbling with the latest news – he had the answer, straight from the horse's mouth. He corrected himself: 'Well, Mrs Hall's mouth.'

'So what is it?' Vinnie asked.

'Let's find Kathleen, so she can hear it as well.'

In doing this, they discovered another mystery, for Kathleen and Joey were arguing in a quiet corner of the playground. 'Come on, out with it, Joey!' Kathleen demanded. 'There's something you're not telling me.'

'Oh, leave me alone.' Joey marched off to his classroom.

Vinnie and Dobbs were puzzled. They'd never once seen Kathleen and Joey have as much as a cross word between them.

Vinnie asked, 'Kathleen, what's wrong?'

She seemed embarrassed. 'Um... Joey and I won't be at school tomorrow. I have to tell the headmaster.' She shrugged in a helpless sort of way and left them.

'Well, what about that?' Vinnie said.

'Looks like I'll have to tell you Mrs Hall's news.' So Dobbs launched into the story. 'We were right, Vinnie! Somebody's nicked old Murdoch's belt.'

'So he'll just get another one.'

'That's the good part. There isn't another belt in the whole school. Mrs Hall heard that Murdoch tried to borrow Miss Fargie's, but she never had one. Told him the evacuees have got away from Hitler's violence, so she's not helping him do more of it.'

'So we were right about what he lost. The question is, *who* nicked it?'

'I thought it was you.'

'Same here, Dobbs, but I didn't like to say.' Vinnie thought for long seconds, then added, 'It should happen to Adolf Hitler.'

✳ ✳ ✳

'I've got an idea, Joey,' Vinnie said as they got off George Preston's bus after school. 'How about we go and watch trains for a while?'

'No thanks. I'm going to my billet.' Joey never called Mrs Watney's house home. Only the happier evacuees did that.

'Well, *I'd* like to look at the trains,' Dobbs persisted. 'Might cheer me up. You as well.'

'They're along that way.'

'But we need you to come with us, Joey,' Vinnie urged. 'Tell us what to look for.'

'They're big black things with wheels on them.

They go *chuff-chuff*. You can't miss them. Anyway, I never want to see a train for the rest of my life.' Joey walked away.

Vinnie and Dobbs exchanged looks. Kathleen shrugged unhappily, then trailed after Joey.

Vinnie said, 'What's got into him?'

Dobbs shook his head. 'Every small boy loves trains. It's natural. Trains and fire-engines. Something's amiss.'

* * *

On Friday morning at breakfast, Kathleen and Joey were surprised to find they each had a boiled egg and butter to spread on their toast. 'I've got a nice bit of bacon here as well,' Mrs Watney added. 'Would you like me to put some on for you?'

Kathleen felt so weak and helpless she could hardly speak. 'No thank you, we'd rather not have bacon.' It was the only way she could take charge of their lives. This sudden generosity from Mrs Watney was like a bribe. Up until now, for breakfast they'd only had dried-egg omelette, mixed up with water, not milk.

The court appearance was to take place at ten o'clock and Kathleen had insisted that she should go, too. Mrs Watney had tried to assure her that she'd look after Joey, but Kathleen had already arranged to have the morning off school.

The night before in their bedroom, she'd attempted to talk with Joey about what had happened, but he'd turned his face to the wall and refused to speak.

'I wish Mum was here,' Kathleen had said. 'She'd get to the bottom of it.'

'Well, she's not here, is she? She's in London being bombed.' And that's all he would say.

After breakfast, the three of them set off for the local courthouse. Kathleen's heart was heavy, but Mrs Watney looked at the sky and said, 'We've got a lovely morning for it.'

* * *

The local court was in a part of Netterfold that Kathleen hadn't visited before. It stood between a council building and the police station and seemed a very forbidding sort of place. Joey was apprehensive, so Kathleen put her arm around his shoulders. This time he didn't shrug it off. Mrs Watney was familiar with the place and led the way inside. She sat on a long bench and folded her arms. 'We wait here till our name's called.'

'Why will they call *our* name?' Kathleen asked.

'Well, it'll really be my name. But Joey will have to come in, too.'

So they sat and waited until an elderly official came out of a room and called, 'Watney.' Then he recognised Mrs Watney and said, 'In you come, then.'

Mrs Watney led the way into the courtroom, and once more she knew where to sit. The magistrate was already seated, at a long table with a woman clerk beside him. Neither of them looked up, but rather continued to talk among themselves. To one side, a man sat with his arms folded. Kathleen had seen him before, at the school: an ARP man who'd come to tell the students how to recognise a butterfly bomb.

He was the warden who had spotted the light from Dennis's window that night, then pounded on the front door.

The clerk stood and read out the charge – on such-and-such a date the defendant, Mrs Iris Watney, had caused a light to be shown from her house, contrary to defence regulations. When the clerk asked, Mrs Watney said she was not guilty.

Then it was the turn of the ARP man, who described how he'd observed a light showing from a front upstairs bedroom window of the house. He had ordered that the light be put out forthwith; after that he had served notice upon the householder, Mrs Iris Watney.

The magistrate listened, then growled unhappily and demanded of Mrs Watney: 'What have you got to say?'

Mrs Watney launched into her story. 'Well, your worship, these days I am so weary, what with looking after two evacuee children as well as my son, Dennis, who works on the railway.'

The magistrate said, 'Many people put up with much worse.'

'But the point is, your worship, one of the evacuee children,' she pointed to Joey, 'went into my son's room and turned on the gaslight. He didn't put the blackout up.'

Kathleen looked at Joey. Something wasn't right.

The magistrate then fixed his gaze on Joey and ordered, 'Stand up, boy.'

Joey hadn't expected this. He got to his feet unhappily. 'Yes, sir.'

'Now, this country's at war,' the magistrate gruffed. 'And the Germans are looking for lights so they can bomb us from their aeroplanes. So how would you like to be the cause of that, eh? A bomb falling on your sister.' He went on sternly, telling Joey he was a thoughtless young fellow. That there was no excuse for such behaviour, so let it be a lesson to him. Almost in the same breath, the magistrate said to Mrs Watney, 'Fined five pounds. Next case.'

Mrs Watney made an annoyed gasp and shook her head in disbelief. Joey seemed to have shrunk inside his collar. He was close to tears, so Kathleen put her arm around his shoulders again as they went outside.

Mrs Watney said, 'I've got to pay the fine. Mind you, it could have been worse, so you did well, Joey. When Mrs Sturgess showed a light, she got forty pounds.'

* * *

They didn't go to school in the end. There was no bus, and Kathleen decided it was too far to walk. She and Joey stayed in Netterfold park for a while instead, until it began to turn colder.

Kathleen remembered something. 'Mrs Watney does her shopping on Friday, so let's go back to our billet.'

Once there, Joey went into Dennis's room and came back to their bedroom with a cardboard box. 'Dennis said I can play with this.' It was a train set.

'Why did he say that, Joey?'

'He just said I can borrow it.' Joey put the box on his bed, then took out the rails and inspected them. They were rusty and buckled and didn't join together properly. The locomotive had a broken spring and wouldn't wind up. The wheels were locked, so he couldn't even push it along the twisted rails. The two wagons in the set had scratched paint and one of them had a wheel missing.

'It's not a patch on the one you have at home, Joey.'

'And it's not a Hornby, either.'

'It's a bit dark in here,' Kathleen said suddenly. She gave Joey a box of matches. 'Why don't you put the light on?'

Joey took the matches and hesitated. 'Um…can you do it, please?'

'Why?' She waited. 'Don't you know how to do it?' Kathleen took the matches from him, reached up and turned on the gas. She lit a match, then held the flame to the mantle. There came a dull *plop* and yellow light glowed. 'You *can't* do it, can you? You can't turn on the gas.'

'No.'

'And it wasn't you who left the light on in Dishonest Dennis's den! You didn't even go into his room, did you?'

'No.'

'But he got you to say you did.' This time Joey didn't answer, but kept his head down, looking at the ugly train set. Kathleen went on, but not unkindly: 'He paid you with that rusty rubbish; oh yes, and we had boiled eggs and butter this morning. Guess what we'll get tomorrow.'

'I want revenge,' Joey said. He started tossing the rails, the locomotive and wagons into the cardboard box.

'Revenge?' Kathleen asked. 'What sort of revenge can you get? It's done now, and Dennis won.'

'I know things about him. So I'll get my revenge – only I need you to help me, Kathleen.' He thought for a moment or two, then added: 'And maybe you could ask Vinnie and Dobbs, too.'

Pat Keely

UNTIL YOUR EYES
GET USED TO
THE DARKNESS,
TAKE IT EASY

LOOK OUT IN THE BLACKOUT

Chapter Twelve
RED-HOT REVENGE

The night was cold and frosty, with a pale moon. Vinnie had never owned much in the way of warm clothes, so he was glad of the woollen pullover Mrs Greenwood had got for him in a jumble sale. He'd pulled the sleeves down over his hands, but even so, the freezing air nipped at his fingers. It was madness, he decided, to leave a warm bed to go trolling about the midnight streets of Netterfold like some kind of cat-burglar.

He reached the meeting spot, at a low wire fence alongside the railway lines. The trains from Netterfold goods yard ran parallel with the road that Vinnie had just come along. This was the place, but there was no sign of Dobbs, Kathleen or Joey.

Vinnie stamped up and down to ward off the cold, but his feet made a noise on the road surface, and they'd all agreed this was supposed to be a hush-hush, top-secret mission. He blew into his fingers to warm them. Through the fence, the railway lines glistened blue and cold in the moonlight.

To find some warmth, Vinnie crouched behind a small bush and waited. There came a sound: somebody coming. He ducked lower, then made out a lanky, hunched-up shape leaving white vapour-breath hanging in the air. It was Dobbs, who asked through chattering teeth, 'So where are they, then?'

'In the Land of Nod, I expect.' Vinnie made a snoring sound and pointed in the direction of Joey and Kathleen's billet.

'What'll we do? Give them five minutes?'

'Might as well.'

'So what's our mission for tonight?'

'They're being mysterious about it. They know something about this Dennis.'

'And that's where we come in?' Dobbs asked.

'Kathleen said they'll explain when they see us. Said it would be an adventure.' Vinnie crouched lower. 'Shh. Somebody's coming.'

'Is it Dennis?'

'No, it's them.' Vinnie waited until Joey's small figure appeared out of the shadows, with Kathleen close behind him. Then he whispered, 'Where have you been?'

'We had to wait till the witch was asleep,' Kathleen explained.

'To keep awake, I read in bed,' Joey informed them.

'That's what I was doing,' Dobbs said with a shiver. 'If you ask me, I should have kept doing it.'

'So where's Dennis?' Vinnie asked.

Kathleen said, 'He's on a late shift and should be home soon. Then he'll come here.'

'First thing we do is wait for a train to come,' Joey announced. 'A *special* train.'

'*Then* what happens?' Dobbs demanded. 'And what about this explanation? Like, what are we doing here?'

There came a distant double *toot-toot* from a locomotive whistle. They heard the rumble and *chuff-chuff-chuff* of an engine moving slowly as it pulled away from the goods yard.

'That's the train. Come on, hide!' Joey scampered across the road, away from the railway lines, and dropped into a shallow ditch. Vinnie, Kathleen and Dobbs followed. They watched the locomotive draw nearer, snorting and blowing steam from its cylinder drain-cocks. Then it happened. The loco slowed almost to a stop, and one of the men on it began throwing large lumps of coal from the tender. The coal hit the ground, bounced through the gaps in the wire fence and came to rest on the roadside. Then the locomotive gathered speed and rattled away, its wagons rumbling behind.

'So that's how Dennis does it!' Kathleen said.

'Three nights a week he comes out here,' Joey

told them with a note of grim triumph. 'I spied on him. Sneaked out one night and followed him.'

Dobbs asked Kathleen, 'You knew about this?'

'I do now.'

'So what's the plan, Joey?' Vinnie asked. 'This red-hot revenge of yours?'

'We chuck the coal back over the fence,' Joey said. 'There's a ditch in there, beside the railway lines. He'll never find it.'

'Yeah, but where *is* this Dennis?' Dobbs was uneasy as they ran back across the road.

Joey found the first lump of coal, but it was too big for him to manage on his own. 'I delayed him,' he explained. 'Let the air out of his tyres.'

'His bike tyres?' Vinnie asked.

'No, he has a barrow sort of thing, on a couple of bike wheels.'

'I wondered where he kept going in the night,' Kathleen said. 'He must get his barrow from the shed, then come along here to collect the coal that's been left for him.'

Joey added, 'He keeps some himself, shares the rest with the men on the engine. I've watched it happen.'

'Sneaky,' Dobbs said. 'Everyone else goes without coal, but he and his mum are nice and warm.'

'But we don't get any of it,' Kathleen complained bitterly. 'We're sent to bed early, and it's freezing in that room.'

'And the bath water's always cold,' Joey grumbled.

'Dennis could be here any minute,' Vinnie warned. 'So let's get the coal shifted.'

They felt around in the grass beside the fence and quickly discovered the other bits of coal. There were six large lumps, enough to fill a wheelbarrow.

Joey had planned things well. The ditch he'd mentioned was on the railway side of the fence, concealed in long grass. Between them, Vinnie, Kathleen and Dobbs gathered all of the heavy lumps. In ten busy minutes, they'd returned a fair weight of coal to railway property and hidden it well. Suddenly Dobbs hissed, 'Somebody's coming.'

They crouched low and heard the persistent *squeak-squeak-squeak* of a wheel that needed oiling. 'That's Dennis,' Joey said. 'And his barrow. Let's get out of sight.'

If they went across the road to their ditch, they'd be seen. Their best chance was to hide along the line of the fence, away from Dennis. The wheel noise grew louder. Keeping low, they ducked away to crouch behind some low gorse bushes. Kathleen whispered, 'Told you it would be exciting.'

Dobbs muttered, 'So was the book I was reading.'

They saw the hunched figure of Dennis, now with his arms out, feeling in the grass for the coal that was no longer there. Then came another sound that sent a chill down Vinnie's spine: a police whistle, unmistakable in the darkness. All four of them were trapped between the police, who were coming from the direction of the railway goods yard, and Dennis, who also heard the whistle. He leapt to his feet and sprinted back towards Netterfold.

'STOP RIGHT THERE!' Into the scene came Constable Breedon, mounted on his police-issue bicycle. It had a single acetylene lamp at the front, hooded because of the blackout regulations. Breedon spotted Dennis and gave chase, pedalling furiously and blowing his whistle.

Seconds later, the constable crashed noisily and painfully into the abandoned barrow. He sprawled on the road, bellowing angry words.

Kathleen whispered, 'Are policemen allowed to use such language?'

'Only when they hurt themselves,' Vinnie said.

Dobbs added, 'Let's get out of here before he spots us.'

Cautiously they emerged from behind their gorse bushes. Breedon was on his feet now, muttering as he inspected the front wheel of his bicycle. He didn't notice Joey and the others creeping away towards the railway goods yard. Dennis was nowhere in sight.

'Now that was a great revenge,' Joey said. 'The best ever. Dennis gets no coal, loses his barrow, and we can go back to bed.'

'Come on, then,' Vinnie urged, 'we'll have to take the long way round. We can't go past Constable Breedon.'

* * *

In the chilly night air, they walked towards the railway goods yard; then took a turn to the right, aiming to double back into Netterfold. Further along the road they saw another two figures, who carried a heavy sack between them. Dobbs whispered, 'What's this? More coal thieving?'

It was a man and a woman. She was having trouble holding her side of the heavy sack. To bear its weight, she had to lean to the right. They heard her say, 'Don't walk so fast, Georgie.'

Vinnie recognised her voice. It was Joan, the maid from Netterfold House. But who was Georgie? The answer came when the man said in a reasonable sort of voice, 'I told you not to grab so much, Joanie. I knew we'd never carry it all.'

They recognised the voice. It was Mr Preston. That George!

Just then Joan stumbled and let her end of the sack fall on the ground. A heavy can rolled out and trundled back along the road towards Vinnie, Kathleen, Dobbs and Joey. They just had time to duck behind a telephone box as the can changed direction, then bounced into the gutter. It landed at their feet.

'Oh, I'm not getting that,' they heard Joan whimper.

'Are you sure?' he asked her. 'It might be pineapple. You like pineapple, Joanie.' He was talking nicely. This wasn't the George – the *Georgie* – they knew!

Joan said, 'I can't be bothered. It's cold. Come on.' Between them, they hefted the sack and made off. The large can was still lying there, outside the telephone box.

Vinnie whispered in a faraway voice, 'Now I know where the custard powder came from.'

'What custard powder?' Kathleen asked.

'The first time I met Joan, she came into the kitchen with packets of custard powder. Said she found them in the garden. She was only trying to put the blame on the vaccy. That's me.'

'They've gone now,' Dobbs said. 'Georgie and Joanie, eh? Who'd have thought it?'

Vinnie picked up the can, which was a large one. By the light of the moon they read the label. It wasn't pineapple, but tinned ham, from America. Vinnie put it under his arm and they headed back to Netterfold.

'What'll we do with it?' Dobbs asked.

'We could have a feast,' Joey suggested. 'To celebrate.'

Kathleen shook her head. 'Joey, we gave the railway back its coal, and you got your red-hot revenge. The ham's not ours, so no feast.'

'Huh! You sound like Mum.'

They walked in silence, hunched against the cold; then Vinnie said, 'We can use the ham another way. Not eat it, but fix things up, tell some people what's what.' He gave the heavy can to Dobbs and said, 'Here, you carry it.'

'Why me?'

'I need to protect my hands from chilblains,'

Vinnie announced grandly, tucking them under his armpits. 'Because when I grow up, I'm going to be a pianist.'

'Right you are, then, maestro. Anything else I can do for you?'

* * *

The four of them continued to walk the streets of Netterfold in the icy darkness, clutching the large tin of stolen American ham. Somewhere about, on his swift and silent bicycle, was Constable Breedon, who'd not be in a good mood. His frame of mind would only be improved if he caught somebody red-handed. Four evacuee kids would do quite nicely, thank you. With such an arrest, he'd save something from this embarrassing night.

'So, what's next?' Dobbs asked. 'Do we get rid of the loot?'

'Don't call it loot,' Vinnie muttered. 'At least not our loot. Let me think.'

'Well, think faster, Vinnie. This is one heavy ham, and my mouth's watering so much I can hardly walk.'

'Must have been a huge, fat old pig,' Joey remarked wistfully. 'When it was alive. I wonder what its name was?'

Kathleen said, 'Dennis.'

They moved on, looking for another right turn that would take them back to the village. Then came the outline of Netterfold Parish Church.

Dobbs pointed. 'We could leave the tin there.'

'Vicars are honest, aren't they?' Joey asked. 'He'd hand it in?'

'Or give it to poor people,' Kathleen suggested.

'If not, he'll be eating ham sandwiches for a fortnight,' Vinnie replied.

The building looked peaceful in the moonlight, standing in the centre of a stone-walled churchyard and surrounded by weathered gravestones. There was a metal gate, then a winding path to the church door.

Dobbs handed over the tin. 'Off you go, Vinnie. We'll stay here and keep watch.' He crouched down against the stone wall. Kathleen and Joey joined him.

Vinnie hesitated. 'I'm not going in there. Place is full of, you know…graves. Dead people.'

'They're all under the ground,' Kathleen whispered in a practical way. 'They're not going to hurt you.'

'So you come, too,' Vinnie said. 'Then they'll not hurt you either.'

Dobbs stood up again. 'Oh, let's all go.'

It was Joey who pushed open the churchyard gate. It gave a long, eerie squeak, a sound that didn't make them feel any braver. Joey led the way, tiptoeing along the path, glancing left and right. The others came behind him, each wary and fearful. If an owl had hooted at that moment, they'd have died on the spot.

Vinnie overtook Joey and reached the main door of the church, where he gently set the tin down, remembering to give it a wipe with his sleeve.

'Fingerprints,' he whispered. Then, as an after-thought, he peeled the paper label off the tin. 'Evidence,' he added, although at that moment he had no idea what he'd do with it.

He was just about to turn back when the latch rattled. All four heard it and stiffened. The church door began to open.

MINISTRY ⓂⒻ OF FOOD

RATION BOO[K]

(JUNIOR)   1944-

Surname............ EDGECOMBE.

Other Names............ K. T.

Address 83 / 6 Christchurch Rd
(as on Identity Card)

.... Boscombe

Date of birth (Day) 22ⁿᵈ (Month) June (Year) 19

NATIONAL REGISTRATION NUMBER	EABK	395: 4

R.B.4 / 7   JUNIO[R]

FOOD OFFICE CODE No.   **J**

Serial No. of Ration Book

E 115010

IF FOUND RETURN TO ANY FOOD OFFICE

Chapter Thirteen
CHANGES

There wasn't time to make it back to the gate, so they scrambled to hide behind the nearest large headstone. Two dark figures came out of the church and closed the door. It was a man and a woman, carrying no light. The woman wept. The man put an arm around her shoulder and said, 'It's hard, lass, but bear up.'

The couple stayed for a second or two, then went off, huddled together, towards a building that stood on the edge of the churchyard. When they had gone, Vinnie and the others were quiet and suddenly serious.

Kathleen whispered, 'What was that about? And who were they?'

'I think I might know. But let's get out of here.'
Dobbs was unusually solemn.

They walked towards Netterfold. Kathleen asked,
'Are you going to tell us, Dobbs?'

'It's freezing. I want to get to bed.'

'At least tell us a bit,' Joey persisted.

'Tomorrow. At school.'

Vinnie said, 'It's like a serial. You get the next
episode later.'

'Huh!' Joey stamped his feet. 'Now I'll never get
to sleep.'

* * *

The next morning, George Preston sat surly at the
wheel of the school bus as usual. Dobbs and Vinnie
waited until Freddie Preston and the other locals
had climbed aboard; then they got on. They'd met
earlier to work out a plan of campaign and wanted
an audience.

Dobbs greeted the driver. 'Morning, George.'

'Eh?' George Preston sat bolt upright. 'To you
vaccies, it's *Mister* Preston.'

'Lots of other things we could call you,' Vinnie
said.

'Prisoner-at-the-bar,' Dobbs suggested, 'or Convict
Ninety-nine.'

George Preston's eyes narrowed suspiciously. He
lowered his voice. 'What are you on about?'

Vinnie showed half of the label he'd peeled from
the tin of American ham. 'This came off the tin Joan

dropped last night.' He paused. 'You were seen, George.'

Dobbs nodded agreement. 'Witnesses, George. Four of us.'

Freddie Preston began to take a keen interest in what was going on at the front of the bus. He couldn't hear what the vaccies were saying – but why wasn't his brother telling them to sit down and shut up?

The driver's eyes swivelled in desperation. 'That label doesn't prove anything.'

'That's not what Joan says,' Vinnie countered.

Dobbs couldn't resist, and added, 'Joanie.'

George Preston was suddenly alarmed. 'You talked to her?'

'Constable Breedon already did,' Dobbs said.

It wasn't true. Neither Dobbs nor Vinnie had caught up with Joan. They moved on and found seats. Then Kathleen and Joey came aboard the bus. 'Morning, George,' Joey greeted the driver cheerfully.

George Preston ignored this familiarity and started the engine, then drove off with a jolt. Kathleen and Joey lurched into their seats, facing Vinnie and Dobbs. All four made the 'V for victory' sign with their fingers, the way Mr Churchill did when he wanted to cheer up the nation.

As soon as the students were off the bus at school, the driver roared away in a cloud of dust. Freddie looked at Vinnie and Dobbs, who shrugged as if to say, *Don't ask us.*

* * *

At the midday break, Kathleen found Vinnie and Dobbs. 'Last night,' she began, 'those two people who came out of the church—'

'Yes,' Dobbs said, becoming serious the way he'd done the night before.

'You know them?' Vinnie asked.

'I'm friends with Mrs Hall's son, Henry,' Dobbs began. 'He's the telegram boy, only he's beginning to hate it.'

The others nodded in understanding. Everyone in Britain knew about telegrams. They were delivered in a small yellow envelope, and in wartime people came to dread their arrival. For those who waited at home for information, telegrams often brought news that a loved one had been wounded or taken prisoner by the enemy.

The worst telegram to receive said, in block capitals: 'THE WAR OFFICE REGRETS TO INFORM YOU...'

'Henry hates delivering them. He goes to the front door, rings the bell, or knocks, whatever. Someone comes and sees him in his uniform. One look's enough; they sort of crumple, hold on to the doorpost for support—'

'They know it could be bad news?' Vinnie asked.

'Or worse news,' Kathleen said.

'Henry has to wait while people read the telegram; then they break down and cry,' Dobbs went on. 'Sometimes they're afraid of that yellow envelope. They say they haven't got their glasses, so they ask

Henry to read it for them. Imagine him having to do that? Then, after giving the bad news, Henry knows they'll be left on their own. He doesn't like to leave them with all that grief, so he runs to find a neighbour. Or someone else to stay with them. After that he goes back to the post office, where there might be another telegram to deliver.'

'And those two last night?' Kathleen prompted.

'The vicar and his wife,' Dobbs said. 'The Reverend Aintree and Mrs Aintree. They got a telegram about their son. One of the worst-news kind.'

* * *

Next day, Vinnie bumped into Joey in the village. Joey had just bought *Dandy* and was walking along reading about Desperate Dan. He was giggling so much he almost literally bumped into Vinnie.

'I could have been a lamppost, young Joey. Then you'd be sorry.'

'I've got news,' Joey said. 'About Dennis.'

'Well, come on. Out with it.'

'He came home from work last night, only he didn't come into the kitchen.'

'And that's it? That's the news?'

'No, wait. Mrs Watney calls him for his tea, and when he comes in, Dennis has got a huge black eye.'

'Who hit him?'

Joey went on, 'I said to him, *Ooh, Dennis, that looks sore. Have you been in a boxing match?* He didn't like that.'

'But *who* hit him?' Vinnie asked again.

'Don't know, but just as Mrs Watney poured his tea, there came a knock at the front door.' Joey was enjoying this tale of retribution. 'It was Constable Breedon, saying he had a barrow down at the police station with DENNIS WATNEY – COAL THIEF on the side.'

Vinnie laughed. 'He was a bit daft, putting that on the barrow.'

'No, I did it before we headed out that night,' Joey explained. 'Part of my revenge plan.'

But the answer to who had given Dennis his black eye had to wait until Dobbs got the delicious information from Mrs Hall: the driver and fireman on the locomotive hadn't believed that Dennis couldn't find the lumps of coal they'd tossed off, so they declared war on him.

'Ouch!' Vinnie said when Dobbs told him, and laughed.

*　*　*

When Friday came, there was no sign of Joan. Mrs Greenwood explained to Vinnie that she'd sent in her notice and gone off to join the Women's Land Army. Vinnie guessed George Preston had warned her, so she'd decided to leave the village.

When Vinnie got on the bus the following Monday, instead of surly George Preston, there was a woman behind the wheel. She wore a cap and a driver's badge. 'Good morning,' she greeted Vinnie cheerfully. 'Bit of a change, seeing me here, eh?'

'Yes, good morning.' He went to sit with Dobbs. 'So where's Georgie?'

'Don't know. But we might ask Freddie.'

The opportunity came at the morning break. Freddie seemed to have something on his mind. He moved towards Vinnie and Dobbs, then changed direction and went somewhere else. Finally, he came over to them and said, 'I want a word.'

'What word's that?' Dobbs asked.

'Um…to say thanks.' Freddie looked down, scuffed one shoe on the ground. 'For my brother.'

'Go on, Freddie.' Vinnie leaned against the school wall.

'You could have made it bad for him. But you didn't. I never knew he was doing all that…you know…'

'Thieving?' Dobbs suggested.

'Yeah, him and Joan. He told Mum before he took off. Anyway, thanks, um, Vinnie and Dobbs. Thanks.'

'So where is he? Where's he gone?' Vinnie asked.

'The Merchant Navy. Signed on as a sailor. In Liverpool.' Then more words poured out of Freddie: 'I hated it, honestly, him driving the bus when he should have been doing real war work. The army or something. I tried to tell him, best way I could, but he didn't listen.'

The bell rang for the end of the morning break.

Vinnie said, 'It's okay, Freddie. Better late than never, eh?'

* * *

Friday afternoons were the best time of the school week, because Mr Murdoch gave the class an hour to do private reading. Without his punishing belt he'd calmed down a little; he remained aloof, but as the days passed the thaw in him was becoming more obvious.

Kathleen had borrowed *We Didn't Mean to Go to Sea* from Netterfold Library. At home in London she had three other Arthur Ransome books and she'd been thrilled to find this one here that she hadn't read. It was good to lose herself in a pre-war story about children who accidentally went to sea in the *Goblin*.

Vinnie read a book on the life of Mozart. At the end of his music lesson the day before, Miss Armstrong had let him borrow it, then changed her mind and said he could keep it. She had written her name in the front long ago, which made it feel even more special to him. The book was fascinating, but heavy going, with whole sentences in German. Vinnie wished Isaac was there to help translate.

Dobbs had a small chess set on his desk, and a book of chess problems. He was stuck on the last one: the black king opposed to the white king and the queen. This one was really difficult. His exasperation showed. At one point he muttered, 'Ach. Stupid!'

Mr Murdoch looked up from his newspaper. 'Using that word in this room is my privilege, boy.'

'Sorry, sir.'

But Mr Murdoch didn't leave it there. He'd seen the chess set and the book. He rose and paced towards Dobbs. 'Problems, eh?' Already his tone had changed.

'Yes, sir.'

Mr Murdoch picked up the book and seemed impressed. 'You've done these? All of them?'

'Except the last one, sir.'

The teacher turned the chess board around and studied it. 'Well, what say we do it as if it's a game? I'll take the black king.' The class stopped reading and looked on with interest. Mr Murdoch said to the boy who sat in the desk next to Dobbs, 'Here, you shift over there.' He sat down himself; then teacher and student pondered the chess board.

A few minutes before the bell rang, Dobbs leaned back and said, 'Checkmate.'

'Fair and square, Dobbs. Fair and square!'

'Thanks for the game, sir.'

Mr Murdoch went back to his desk and folded his newspaper. 'I must say,' he went on, 'your English has improved, lad. Not a hint of an accent.' But he was smiling.

✳ ✳ ✳

It was Dobbs who brought about another change. When Christmas mail arrived in the post office, he'd help Mrs Hall to sort it. One day, he noticed a parcel from London addressed to Kathleen and Joseph Pearson, care of Mrs Watney. Not knowing about Kathleen's arrangement for letter collection, he put the parcel in the mailbag for the postwoman to deliver.

Two days later, at school, Dobbs asked, 'How'd you and Joey like your parcel, Kathleen?'

Kathleen looked blank. 'Parcel?'

'You didn't get it, then?' He used his hands to show how wide and tall the parcel had been. 'You'll have to ask Witch Watney about it.'

'Soon, Dobbs.' Kathleen couldn't hide her dismay, or her reluctance. 'I'll do it soon. Thanks for telling me.'

That night at tea, Dobbs casually passed on the story to Mrs Hall, who became very interested in this piece of news. 'Interfering with the Royal Mail is a *very* serious matter. Leave it with me, Dobbs.'

That was all it took. From then on, things moved swiftly. Mrs Ormsby-Chapman, the billeting officer, hammered on Mrs Watney's door, then stated her case: 'Three days ago a Christmas parcel was delivered here, Mrs Watney, addressed to the evacuee children in your care.'

'Oh, yes,' Mrs Watney agreed. 'I'm keeping it for them, for Christmas morning.'

'Then may I see the parcel?'

'Oh.'

'I take it you can't produce it? In an unopened condition?'

'Well—'

'Mrs Watney, I am not satisfied that you are fit to

have children in your care. I believe you also had the younger one of them in court, before my husband, the magistrate. Without the approval of the boy's parents.'

'But—'

'You have interfered with their mail, and I am not satisfied that they are receiving their proper rations. The postal authorities will investigate further and the children will be removed from this place. Good day to you.'

When Kathleen and Joey got off the bus from school, Mrs Ormsby-Chapman was there to meet them with her car. They collected their possessions from Mrs Watney's unhappy house and were swept away to stay with the vicar and his wife, the Reverend and Mrs Aintree.

'Do you like trains?' the Reverend Aintree asked Joey. 'Well, you shall sleep in my son's bedroom. Now there was a boy who was absolutely mad about them.'

'Hornby trains?' Joey asked hopefully.

'Oh yes, Hornby,' the Reverend Aintree replied. 'And not clockwork, either.'

Mrs Aintree hugged Kathleen and smiled. 'It'll be lovely having you here.'

Chapter Fourteen
A German

It was summer, and Vinnie and Miss Armstrong were in the middle of a piano lesson. The windows were open and the afternoon scent of flowers filled the music room. Vinnie played a Mozart piece, 'Twinkle, Twinkle Little Star'. Isaac had enjoyed it, adding endless variations to the original simple nursery tune, making the pub customers smile and ask for more. Now it was Vinnie's turn, but the second variation was as far as he'd progressed. He finished playing and looked at Miss Armstrong.

She shook her head slowly and made a doubtful face. 'M-mm, it was *fairly* good, I suppose. But it's a lullaby, Vinnie, to make babies sleep, not a marching tune for the Grenadier Guards. So, again please, and softer. Lull me.'

He began to play from the beginning and risked a glance to see what she thought of it so far. She did not look soothed, so he played on, putting as much *legato* into the music as he could. Then came a sound, a heavy drone overhead that grew louder with every moment.

'Bombers!' Vinnie leapt from his seat. His face was white. 'Miss Armstrong, it's an air raid!'

But she sat still, quite composed. 'I think they're on our side, Vinnie.'

Now he could hear them properly, he realised the drone was a steady one, not *voom-ah*, *voom-ah* as he remembered.

He nodded, relieved. 'Yes, ours.' Vinnie went to the window and looked up. There were trees outside in the garden, so he only caught glimpses of the aircraft through the leaves and upper branches.

Miss Armstrong said, 'As long as that's going on we won't be able to hear any twinkling. Why don't you go outside and watch them?'

'Thank you, yes.'

To have a clear view of the sky, Vinnie had to walk into the middle of the street. Overhead he saw a formation of lumbering Halifax bombers, almost darkening the afternoon summer sky as they flew towards Germany. The aircraft came in waves, one group receding eastwards as another approached from the west. The roar of the engines didn't let up, even when the sky was empty.

At last, with no aeroplanes to see and the sound gone, he went back to the music room. 'Imagine that lot coming to bomb you.'

'Yes, Vinnie, and many of the young crewmen will not return. Imagine that.'

Following such an experience, it didn't seem right to play something so lighthearted. Instead they went over the sheet music, marking the passages that should be played softly and more lyrically.

* * *

In Netterfold, the late summer days of 1941 were glorious. It had been a good harvest in the fields around the village, with everyone lending a hand to gather the corn or dig up potatoes. In August, the school gave an extra week of holidays so that older students could help with the work. After it was over, Vinnie, Dobbs, Kathleen and Joey leaned on a gate looking at an empty field where they'd laboured under the hot sun.

All four of them were red in the face, arms and legs, but they had a sense of satisfaction. They each sucked straws, in what they thought was proper country style.

'Ar,' Dobbs imitated a farmer. 'Oi reckon, next season, oi shall put in mangel wurzels. You loikes mangel wurzels, don't ee, Kath lass?'

'Oh, I do. Oi likes them in soup, oi do.'

'Come on, yokels, let's walk.' Vinnie opened the gate and went on into the field. Joey, now wise to country ways, carefully shut the gate after them.

They knew there was a small brook on the far side of the field where they could take off their shoes and sandals, then paddle in the cool water. But before they even reached the middle of the field, there came the sound of an aircraft.

It wasn't a British one this time – they could tell by the engine sound and the markings on the wings and tailfin. The plane was in trouble, the motor coughing and missing badly. It trailed oily smoke from just behind the propeller.

'It's a Focke Wulf!' Dobbs yelled. 'A Jerry!' Most boys knew the outline of German aircraft from government posters. 'Dive for cover!' He looked for somewhere to hide, but the field was wide and flat.

'No, wait!' Joey shouted. 'There's a Spitfire chasing it!' The British plane roared after the German aircraft, but it wasn't firing its guns. It had already hit the Focke Wulf, and the air-force pilot needed no more than to follow and mark where the Focke Wulf would crash-land.

Quite suddenly, the canopy of the German aeroplane flew back and the pilot jumped out. His parachute hesitated for a second or two before billowing open; then the man began floating down towards them.

Joey cried, 'Come on, let's capture the Jerry!' He made a dash towards where he expected the German to land, all the while looking upwards to check that the pilot was on course.

Kathleen screamed in fear, 'Joey, no! Don't!' She followed after him, yelling, 'He might have a gun! Don't go near him!'

Joey didn't listen, but ran faster, jumping over the uneven ground.

Both aircraft disappeared behind a line of trees. Seconds later came a loud crash as the Focke Wulf hit the ground. Vinnie and Dobbs sprinted across the field behind Kathleen and Joey. They got there just as the pilot hit the ground with a painful *thump*, then rolled awkwardly on the stubbly earth. His parachute floated after him and gently settled. The pilot called to them in English, 'Don't shoot.' But he smiled in relief as he said the words, recognising these were children.

'Hands up!' Joey ordered.

'Only one hand,' the pilot said and held up his right. 'The other one is not so good anymore.'

Kathleen was fascinated and horrified at the same time. Here was a German, who'd come in his aeroplane to do damage, to kill, then fly back and maybe brag about what he'd done. She held on to Joey's shoulders to stop him moving any closer to the man. Vinnie and Dobbs, panting, stood undecided.

Kathleen asked the pilot, 'Are you hurt?' She'd spoken her first words to the enemy; words of care.

'This arm and this leg.' The German showed them his left side. 'I will not be very nimble with the walking, so I'll rest here awhile.' He looked at the blue sky and the peace that was all around. He nodded. 'Beautiful.' The German had fair hair and piercing blue eyes and didn't seem at all dangerous or menacing.

'Do you want us to get help?' Vinnie asked.

'No, I think your people will be here soon enough,' the pilot said. 'Your countryman in the Spitfire will already have reported me. I shall wait.' He looked at them and smiled again. 'So what are your names?'

'I don't think we should tell you,' Joey said. 'It's secret information.'

'What if I promise not to tell the German High Command?' The pilot solemnly crossed his heart. So one by one, they told him their names. He nodded and said, 'My name is Helmut Bergman, and I am honoured to meet you. As you can see, my war is over now.'

'But you're still alive,' Dobbs said. 'The war's over for a lot of people – everything's over for them. I know because I see the telegrams.'

'Then, Dobbs,' the pilot said, 'when you grow older, you must never make war, never fight, but do a lot of talking. Talking's good, war is not.'

There came a cry from the gate where they'd entered the field. 'Get away from him! You people, get away from that filthy Hun!'

'Filthy Hun, eh?' The pilot was amused. 'Someone has been reading *Biggles*. Oh yes, in Germany we have heard of your Biggles.'

Two red-faced boys came racing across the field,

leaving the gate open. One was the well chosen Ralph DuPreis, the other his friend from the train.

Joey recognised them. 'It's Lord Snooty.'

'Where have *they* been?' Kathleen almost snorted the words.

'Not helping get the spuds in,' Dobbs muttered. 'I know that much.'

'I said, get away,' Ralph shouted as he ran. He and his friend were dressed in white shorts, shirts and canvas running shoes without socks. Ralph stopped only to pick up a large stick; then he arrived on the scene, out of breath. He said, 'Hands up, you!'

'His arm's broken,' Kathleen said reasonably, 'And the army will be here.'

Joey added, 'And we found him first.'

Ralph ignored this and stared hard, breathing noisily, thrusting his chest forward. Then he seemed to steel himself. He lifted the stick and made an angry swing at the pilot. 'This is for Dunkirk—!'

Dobbs caught Ralph by the wrist, took the stick away from him and tossed it aside. 'Don't be a fool, Ralphie. Now why don't you and your chum just keep running?'

'German-lover! Nazi-lover!' Ralph spat the words. 'He should be shot!' Then he stumped off across the field.

His friend gasped, 'I say,' hesitated for a second or two, and followed Ralph.

The pilot said, 'See, Dobbs. Talk is everything. Even angry talk.'

'Army's here,' Vinnie said.

Six older men in steel helmets and military uniform came across the stubble. They carried rifles with bayonets fixed, but were in no particular hurry. Nor were they part of the regular army; they were Home Guard men. The first thing one of them said when they arrived was, 'That's a nice bit of parachute silk.'

The corporal with them suggested, 'Better nab it then, Alf, before the air force gets here.'

Kathleen explained, 'Mr Bergman can't stand, or put his hands up. He's injured.'

'Mr Bergman, eh?' The first Home Guard man shook his head. 'Charming bugger's only been here a couple of minutes.'

The Home Guard men were relaxed and amiable. This wasn't the first German they'd met since the war began. Three nights ago a Heinkel bomber had crash-landed six miles away in Duffton; the crew had been captured.

Helmut Bergman said, 'Maybe you should go away now, Kathleen and Joey, Vinnie and Dobbs. Not stay here.'

They drew back a little way while one of the Home Guard rolled up the discarded parachute. The others crouched in a circle around the pilot. The corporal asked, 'You got a gun on you, Fritz?'

'It is still in my aircraft.' The pilot waved his good hand. 'All gone.'

A camouflaged lorry came bouncing across the

field, and everyone paused. 'Oi, oi,' one of the Home Guard observed without humour. 'Here comes the air force. Grabbing all the bloody glory for themselves.'

'Good thing, too,' the corporal said. 'Means we don't have to carry him.'

Four Royal Air Force men jumped out of the lorry. An officer with them saluted Helmut Bergman, who responded, but not with the 'Heil Hitler' stiff-armed salute. The air-force men were matter-of-fact about what they had to do. In seconds they produced a stretcher, then carefully loaded their German prisoner into the lorry and climbed aboard themselves.

The last Vinnie, Kathleen, Dobbs and Joey saw of Helmut Bergman was the smile and the wink he gave them. He called, 'Remember to talk.' Then an air-force man put the tailgate up and jumped in and the lorry drove off.

The Home Guard men trudged off to stand guard over the wrecked Focke Wulf while Vinnie, Kathleen, Dobbs and Joey went across the field to the brook. And there, barefoot, they splashed away the rest of the summer afternoon.

Dobbs eventually clambered out of the water and sat on the bank, drying his feet with a handful of grass. 'He was ordinary,' he said at last, 'that German pilot. Just an ordinary man.'

'That's what war is,' Kathleen agreed. 'Ordinary people fighting other ordinary people. And I don't suppose most of them really want to. *They've* got houses, jobs, wives and children. So have we.'

Vinnie got out of the brook and began rubbing his ankles with some grass. 'What if,' he began slowly, 'and I don't mean in this war, I mean maybe in ten years or twenty years from now, what if the government said we're going to war?'

Kathleen took it up. 'And what if everybody said, no, we're not going to do it?'

Dobbs added, 'So everybody tells them to talk some more about it. Okay?'

Vinnie said, 'So, if they want a war, they can fight it themselves.'

After a long pause, Joey held up a finger and asked, 'But we still get to wear uniforms – right?'

The others put their shoes on and trudged back across the field to their homes in Netterfold.

Goodnight children
—everywhere

Never still for a moment. What
energy they use! Now it's time
for that long refreshing sleep—a
cup of hot OXO and off to bed.

OXO

Prepared from
PRIME RICH BEEF

Chapter Fifteen
TWO SUNDAYS AND A MONDAY — 1943

On the first Sunday, Dobbs pedalled past Netterfold Parish Church, where the morning service was in progress. This was the only day of the week Henry in the post office didn't need the bike, so Dobbs could take it for a spin. Regulations stated that bicycles were not to be used for private purposes. 'In other words,' Mrs Hall warned, 'you can ride the post-office bike, but don't let anybody see you.'

'Fat chance of that,' Dobbs had said. 'It's painted red, and I'm the tallest boy in the village!'

As he passed the church gates, the front wheel of the bike started dragging more than usual. He got off and gave the tyre a press with his thumb.

Tom Bradley came by, seated high on his father's oversized bike, his toes barely touching the pedals. 'What's up, Dobbs?'

'Tyre's soft as a jelly.'

'Pump it up then.'

'Pump's useless. Washer's gone.'

Tom circled around, then dismounted to examine the problem. 'I tell you what. I've got a bit of something in the shed. You can make a new washer. That'll do the trick.'

There came a sudden crashing volume of sound from the open front door of the church. It was the organ, blaring out the opening chords of 'Onward, Christian Soldiers'.

'Hell's bells!' Dobbs stood wide-eyed at this attack on his eardrums. 'Glad I'm out here, not in there with that racket.'

'That's Miss Mimms,' Tom explained. 'Deaf as a brick. She plays the organ like billy-o. Come on, I live along there.'

They wheeled their bikes to the old garden shed around the back of Tom's house. It was an Aladdin's cave of old garden tools, spades, hoes, broken machinery and derelict bits and pieces. Rust and mildew were on the attack and spiders reigned. There was even a black cast-iron kettle with its broken-off spout lying alongside it. 'Dad's going to fix that one day,' Tom said.

In the middle of the shed was a solid wooden bench, which had an ancient vice attached to it with square-headed bolts. Tom unclipped the pump from the post-office bike, then with a few expert twists he took it apart. He showed what was left of the pump washer. 'Seen better days.' Tom flicked it into a rubbish box, then started laying out the tools he'd need for the repair job – a large wooden mallet and a circular metal punch. From a drawer he casually produced a leather belt and flapped it lengthwise on the bench.

Dobbs thought this particular piece of leather looked somehow familiar. 'Um, Tom, isn't that…?'

'Yeah, old Murdoch's belt.'

'So it was you who nicked it?'

'No, I confiscated it. See, you vaccies were bombed out of London and lots of folk here were against you from the start. Once I got to know you, I thought it was a bit much. So when the teacher was laying into you as well, I couldn't have that. Live and let live, eh? That's what Dad says, and he was gassed at the Somme.'

'Gee.' Dobbs was touched. 'Thanks, Tom. But you should have mentioned it at the time!'

'It wasn't a time for saying things. It was a time for doing. That's what mattered.' Tom took the circular punch in one hand and the mallet in the other. 'Here goes, then.' He placed the punch on the belt and gave the other end a fierce whack with the mallet. Then he showed a perfect circle of leather, which neatly fitted the tube of the pump. 'A bit of linseed oil on that and it'll work a treat.'

Dobbs held the belt up and looked at Tom through the hole he'd created. 'If old Murdoch could see it now.'

'Best use that was ever made of it,' Tom said.

The pump with its new washer worked beautifully, and Dobbs said thanks again, then went on with his Sunday run. The church was silent, but as he passed the front door another thunderous organ barrage made him swerve.

'Hell's bells!'

The tune was 'Jerusalem'.

* * *

Kathleen was suffering. The sound of Miss Mimms playing on the Netterfold Parish Church organ almost physically hurt her ears. The congregation did its best to sing along, but no voice could be heard above those crashing chords.

> *And did those feet in ancient time*
> *Walk upon England's mountain green?*

Finally the worshippers sang the last of the words:

> *Till we have built Jerusalem*
> *In England's green and pleasant land.*

Miss Mimms continued blaring out the music for another verse, yet nobody told her to stop.

Joey put his hands over his ears and pressed his lips together to stop them smiling. Kathleen tried to catch the Reverend Aintree's eye, but he stared ahead, drumming his fingers on the brass rail around the pulpit. At last the music ended, and with a final blessing from the vicar, the parishioners returned to the peace of their homes.

Kathleen and Joey had begun attending the Sunday service when they moved into the vicarage. In London, their mother had always said they could decide on religion for themselves when they were older, and the Reverend and Mrs Aintree didn't apply any pressure either.

Joey enjoyed the hymns and Kathleen liked the serenity of the old church building, with its dark varnished pews, rough-hewn stonework and stained-glass windows. The date '1643' was carved above the main door, making her picture the people who'd come here over those years.

What would they think of the events of 1943?

After the service, the Reverend and Mrs Aintree gathered Kathleen and Joey, then went across the churchyard to the vicarage.

'Oh, dear,' the vicar sighed. 'My ears are still ringing. What am I going to do about Miss Mimms?'

'Charles, you must tell her,' Mrs Aintree pleaded.

Joey added, 'Her noise broke one of the stained-glass windows.'

'No, Joey, a bird did that,' the Reverend Aintree laughed. 'We mustn't be uncharitable.' He shook his head. 'Problem is, there's no other organist.'

'Um…' Kathleen began. 'I know a boy who plays the piano. He's very good.'

'But we don't want to hurt Miss Mimms' feelings,' Mrs Aintree said. 'She's played the organ here since the early twenties.'

'Not *her* early twenties,' the vicar added. 'They were much earlier again.'

Kathleen persisted: 'Could you ask Miss Mimms to give this boy a try-out?'

'Yes, I see how that would work.' The vicar became thoughtful. 'She takes him under her wing?'

Joey said, 'And lets him play all the loud hymns, but softly.'

'So, Kathleen, what's the name of this boy?'

* * *

Vinnie had discovered the Weeks. The war cost money, and to raise it the army, navy or air force held displays to show their work to the public. On the Sunday when Kathleen and Joey were risking their hearing and Dobbs was finding a new use for a leather belt, Vinnie went to a Royal Air Force display.

It was a mix of photographs of action in the air and a chance to see a Hurricane fighter up close. People queued to pay threepence, then were allowed to sit in the cockpit. When it came his turn, Vinnie discovered it was very cramped inside.

Pride of place in the Royal Air Force display was a Heinkel bomber that a British fighter pilot had shot down a few miles away. The German aircraft looked a sorry sight, its fuselage peppered with bullet holes, the twin propellers bent backwards.

Vinnie stood awe-struck. *Did one of these kill you, Isaac? Did this thing, or one of its brothers, blow away Mr and Mrs Rosen, the pub and all the dreams we used to have?*

Freddie Preston broke unwelcome into his thoughts. 'Not so frightening now, eh?'

Vinnie hid his annoyance. 'But they still are, Freddie. Plenty more bombers up there.'

Freddie ignored this and wandered around to the back of the Heinkel. He called, 'Hey, look what's all over the tailfin.'

The Nazi swastika symbol had almost been covered with National Savings Stamps.

Mrs Hall called out from a nearby post-office stall, 'Come on, Vinnie. Do your bit for the war effort. Buy a stamp and help hide that swastika. You too, Freddie.'

Vinnie had tuppence-ha'penny left and Freddie had the rest, so they found a bare patch on the tailfin and stuck on their sixpenny savings stamp. Freddie tried to add up the amount of money that was already stuck up there, but lost count at twenty-three pounds and some shillings.

Vinnie said, 'I'm heading home now, Freddie.'

'There's more to see. Lots more.'

'Well, you look at it and tell me tomorrow.' He started walking. It gave him time to think.

* * *

Later in the afternoon, Miss Mimms was seated at the organ, but not playing. Vinnie entered the church and approached from behind. He coughed, but she paid no attention. Then he remembered Kathleen telling him that the organist was hard of hearing.

He moved to her side so she could see him. Miss Mimms smiled. 'Ah, you must be the famous Vinnie.'

'Don't know about famous.'

'Well, Vinnie, this is the organ, keys, pedals and stops.' She went on without a break, showing how to switch on the electric blower, skimming through the sheet music for a hundred and one hymns, then invited him to sit and play something.

He played the accompaniment for two hymns: 'Onward, Christian Soldiers', followed by 'Jerusalem'. Vinnie loved the way this different sound made by the organ soared around the old church.

Miss Mimms smiled. 'You'll do, Vinnie. You'll do very well. Now, a secret. I've wanted to give up for a while, so to give the vicar a nudge, I started doing... naughty things. And nobody seemed to notice, even when I played at full volume.'

'M-mm.' He'd heard a different story.

'Now, Vinnie. Are you free on Sunday mornings? For the duration of the war?'

'Well, yes.'

'Excellent. You are now the organist of Netterfold Parish Church. Good luck.'

And with that, Miss Mimms took her handbag and left. Vinnie smiled. *Just what I wanted. Playing in front of an audience. Not like it was in the pub, but the same idea.*

Since he had the church to himself, he tried out 'Kiss Me Goodnight, Sergeant Major', then followed it with 'Bless 'em All'.

* * *

On the second Sunday, at lunch in the vicarage, the Reverend Aintree was full of good humour. The new organist's first service had been a success, with many nods of approval from the congregation.

'Mind you,' the vicar bubbled with amusement, 'I'd love to hear Vinnie give us *Knees Up, Mother Brown*. Wouldn't it shake them up?'

In the midst of the laughter around the dining-room table, the telephone rang. Mrs Aintree went out to the hall to answer it, then called out, 'Kathleen, dear, it's for you. Your mother, ringing from London.'

Kathleen took the receiver. A phone call was unusual, and worrying. She whispered, 'Hello, Mum.'

'Kathleen, darling, I have some bad news.' Her mother paused, made a small gasp. 'About your father.' Then her words came in a rush. 'His ship has been…torpedoed. In the Atlantic Ocean. About five hundred miles from Ireland.'

'Oh.' Kathleen's knees felt suddenly weak. 'Is there any…I mean…'

'Not yet. His tanker was in a convoy. There are – were – Royal Navy ships around, so there's hope.'

'I wish I could be with you, Mum.'

'I too.'

'Have you moved back into our house?'

'No, not really. As I said, it was badly damaged.'
Again she paused. 'It had to be pulled down. The
whole street was hit. Sorry, darling.'

'Our things?'

'There was fire, too. So.' Her mother sounded
tearful. 'I'll let you know more as soon as I hear,
and Kathleen, give Joey a hug from me as you tell
him about Daddy. Darling, I'm calling from a public
telephone box. It's the only one in the street that's
still working, and there's a queue.'

'Yes, you must give others a chance. Bye, Mum. I
love you.'

'You, too. And Joey.'

Kathleen hung up and found Mrs Aintree at
the living-room door. 'That was a bad-news call,
Kathleen? Yes?'

Kathleen could only nod. Mrs Aintree held her
arms wide, the best thing she could have done.

* * *

On Monday morning, Henry Hall delivered the
telegram to the Reverend Aintree, who opened
it, although it was addressed to Kathleen. Henry
waited to see if there was to be a reply. Instead the
vicar said, 'Let me have your bicycle, Henry. I'll
bring it back later.'

Kathleen and Joey had insisted on going to
school, saying they weren't the only ones to receive
bad news.

The Reverend Aintree also borrowed Henry's

bicycle clips, then swung his leg over the saddle and pedalled off. He owned a car and was allowed a petrol ration for it, because of his work. But the tyres were quite bald, so it was dangerous to drive.

Mr Boyce, the headmaster, had assembled the entire school in the hall to give a lecture on the danger of unexploded bombs. Joey had somehow left his own class group to work his way closer to Kathleen.

All the windows in the school had been reinforced against bomb blasts with criss-cross strips of sticky brown paper. Even so, it was possible to see through the glass, which was how Kathleen saw the vicar pedalling into the school grounds.

Her heart gave a leap and she hugged Joey. It seemed to take an age before the Reverend Aintree burst into the hall.

Kathleen stood and asked, 'Is there news?'

The vicar waved the yellow envelope. 'The best.'

CHILDREN'S NEWSPAPER

Wartime Issue—2d

POSTAGE
Inland ½d
Abroad ½d

Number
1143

EDITED BY ARTHUR MEE

THE MAPS ARE CHANGING FAST

Spring Is Coming and Summer Is Not Far Behind

THE year of fate moves on, and the complicated chessboard of the world is a maze of riddles. The strangest riddle of all perhaps is that with nineteen-twentieths of the world longing for a quiet life, the odd twentieth can plunge mankind into grievous catastrophe.

Watchtower of Freedom

The solving of that riddle is one of the things that must come with peace; the one thing sure as the daffodils are peeping through this year is that the pieces of the chessboard are ▒▒▒▒▒▒▒ ▒▒▒▒▒ ▒▒ ▒▒▒ direction, that the positions are becoming clearer, and that nothing is hopeless, nothing leads us to despair.

He who sees far knows that the world is moving to a harmony that it has never known. It is a bewildering scene, and there will be much tribulation, but through the dark valley is the light at the end.

SPRING is coming with the glory in which Nature clothes our Island, and it will lift up our hearts to think the bluebells and the tulips and the daffodils have found the Island standing where it did, the Watchtower of Freedom, the citadel of the spiritual heritage of mankind. When the roses bloom again a year will have passed since Hitler thought he had won the war and called in his jackal to pick up some of the pieces of the carcase. But the bubble has burst, the invincible Nazi is no more. In his place is the skeleton at the feast, and black shadows of pestilence and famine creeping about the wilderness. The map has changed indeed, but we do right to be thrilled by the way it changes.

What Shall He Do Now?

Safe in his impenetrable fastness at Berchtesgaden, Hitler must have many maps. What is he to do now? Where shall he strike next? Shall he march on to the East and challenge Russia, Turkey, Arabia, Syria? Shall he march on Palestine and overthrow the Holy Land, setting up the swastika on the Mount of Olives? Shall he seize India in his stride, picking up the oil mines on the way to feed his shrinking stores, and join hands with Japan, ending the China War for her and perhaps throwing in the Australians—who are being an intolerable nuisance? Or shall he turn West instead and overrun this Island? Or shall he look about and put down these rebellions which are bringing down the New Order before it is set up? Or shall he fly to the Mediterranean and sink the British ▒▒▒▒▒▒▒▒▒▒▒ and grind the Rock to powder. With so many miracles for his magic wand to work life must be hard for a conqueror.

Hitler and His Maps

There will be on his wall the map showing him as the lord of the world, with his finger on the coastline from the Arctic, past Norway, Denmark, Holland, Belgium, and France as far as the borders of Spain, covering the English Channel and facing the broad Atlantic. There will be the map of the Balkans with Hungary under his heel, Rumania ready to be kicked to bits, Yugo-Slavia and Bulgaria not so certain to be kicked to bits, and Greece like a granite rock on which the small wheel of the Axis grinds itself to pieces.

THERE will be a map of Asia with the shadow of a great black paw for Russia, and the ancient Turks with their youth renewed, waiting, watching, ready and unafraid.

Skulking Ships and Running Troops

There will be a map of the Mediterranean with little pagan symbols for Nazi domination everywhere, with Mussolini's thousand miles of coastline and his brave ships capturing Egypt and controlling Suez; but will there be, we wonder, another map more true, with Egypt safe and sound, with the brave ships hiding, skulking, or submerged, with Fascist flags pulled down and Australian caps put in their place, with the tragic procession of a hundred thousand starving prisoners, with Italy swept out of sight on her own sea and running hard in her own deserts?

There will be a map of Africa, but will it show, we wonder, Haile Selassie back among his people chasing the Italian troops, Eritrea passing from Italian hands, the South Africans marching from Kenya, and the great French, Belgian, and British highway open to freedom from coast to coast?

THERE will be a map of Spain, which was long ago to have been fighting on the Nazi side, though this conqueror of the world forgot that a country with a sterile interior and a very long coastline must have sea power on its side.

At the Moat

And there will be a map, we may be sure, of a speck of an island so often lost in the mists of the North Sea. This is all he must conquer now, and yet ▒▒▒▒▒▒▒▒ ▒▒▒▒▒▒▒▒▒ sleep at night ▒▒▒▒▒ the Island troubles him.

A stupid and old-fashioned place it is, meddling along, blocking the path of the young nations of the earth, yet its ghosts haunt him by night and its planes by day. It breaks his dreams and plants new hope in every country underneath his heel. It smashes his power at its source, blows up his oil stores; explodes his munitions, paralyses his railways, shatters his power station, breaks up his aerodromes; and for every little child he kills in England it drops a bomb on his war factories.

HE has twice as many men as the Island. If had masses of arms when the Island had none. He came up to its moat with millions of men and thousands of tanks and mechanised powers such as the world had never seen, and at the moat he stands, a last foe in front of him, his wilderness behind him, his eyes filled with the murmuring of a starving multitude, rising and rebellious, remembering perhaps that Napoleon stood there.

Behind the White Cliffs

Then this small Island was alone, yet Napoleon did not cross the moat. Now she is not alone. With her is the greatest empire Liberty ever made and the greatest, republic existing under the sun, and behind the Island's white chalk cliffs are

Continued on page 2

The New Chie

Lord Somers, successor to B-P ▒
Great Britain, splicing a rope ▒

A Lost World's ▒

IN the farthest mountain range of Venezuela rises the Lost World of Auyan-tepui, from which an expedition led by Dr G. H. Tate, of the American Museum of Natural History, has returned to tell of its wonders. On this isolated block of rock, 20 miles long and half as broad, no man lives or has ever lived, and from a gap in its 8000-feet cliffs comes down the highest waterfall in the world. The expedition measured its fall as at least 3300 feet, and probably 5000, and it is named the Angel waterfall from the name of its discoverer, Jimmy Angel.

The tale of its finding is as strange as anything in this strange lost world of Auyan-

tepui ▒▒▒ had h▒ this a▒ nos : Jimmy ▒ aeropla▒ him a▒ mount▒ lost t▒ among▒ prospe▒ He i▒ with r▒ back ▒ prospe▒ rock fr▒ shortly ▒ Angel ▒ gold d▒ the A▒ found ▒

Chapter Sixteen
MAY, 1945

Late on a Saturday afternoon two years later, Vinnie came into the kitchen of Netterfold House. Mrs Greenwood looked up. 'So, how was your wedding?'

'Oh, sort of emotional. More than the others.'

'That must have been, let me see, your fourth? Or fifth?'

'Fifth. The bride's a welder at Gibbinsons. She looked nice.'

'Nice? That's all you can say, is it? The girl goes around begging clothing coupons from all and sundry so she can look her best, and you say she was – nice.'

'You know what I mean. The groom was invalided

out of the Royal Engineers. Lost a leg, but no way was he going to sit through their wedding ceremony, or use crutches. She supported him, and that was amazing.'

'Ah, well.' Mrs Greenwood busied herself at the kitchen table for a moment. 'Yes, Vinnie, one way or another, they're coming back, the men and the women.'

'And flags are everywhere,' Vinnie agreed. At first it had been one family put one out to welcome their own soldier home. Then another household did it. Their flags stayed up, and now it was the whole village.

'All of Britain will be like that. And no more blackout.'

Vinnie made for the kitchen door. 'I'll just put my music away, Mrs Greenwood, then give you a hand here.'

'No, Vinnie, Miss Armstrong has asked to see you.'

'We're not having a lesson, are we? Not on Saturday?'

'Well, go and find out. Don't keep the woman waiting.'

*　*　*

Miss Armstrong greeted him warmly from her chair. 'Come in, Vinnie. You played well for the wedding?' Then without waiting for his reply, she went on, 'Of course you did. Of course you performed well. So, sit, and let's talk.'

He sat at the Steinway, but more nervously than he usually did. *I've been at ease here, in her music room. She has given me confidence; I am not who I was.* There had been times Miss Armstrong just sat nodding as he played. That made him secure. *I am here and this is mine.* Sometimes she closed her eyes and listened, only murmuring a gentle instruction: '*Legato*, Vinnie, that passage, *legato*.'

Miss Armstrong said, 'Well, Vinnie, it would be so easy for you to stay here. I've enjoyed being your mentor over these years. You have repaid me in ways that you'll never realise, nor can I properly explain.'

Vinnie knew there was a 'but' coming. He'd been dreading this. For weeks now, as the war moved to an end, it had begun to hang over him. Every Allied victory made it more certain.

In this room they'd laughed together, teased each other, such as when he'd added a postman's knock at the end of a Mozart *rondo*.

And at times they'd flared up in sudden frustration. 'What are you?' she'd once demanded. 'A pianist in the making, or some honky-tonk pub tinkler?'

'Used to be,' Vinnie had snapped back. 'It's where I came from.'

'Well, you're not there now. And don't forget it!'

So they'd simmer, Vinnie at her piano, Miss Armstrong in her chair, her hopeless hands grasping the walking stick. Then, without being asked, Vinnie would play, and when he was well in command of the piece, he'd say over the music, 'I'm sorry.'

And he'd known there was a 'but' to come, so he said it now: 'But you want me to go?'

'You *have* to go, Vinnie. You have outgrown your mentor. It is what happens to those with talent. Your friend Isaac was your first mentor; I've been your second. And as you progress in music, you will outgrow others. It's a natural thing. And that time has come.'

'I thought it would go on. Here, I mean.'

'This is a backwater. You need to be in the middle of things.' Miss Armstrong showed him a letter. 'I had Mrs Greenwood type this, Vinnie. And if you knew what an effort it was between us.' She cleared her throat. 'It's to a man in London. His name's on the envelope—'

'Will he have a piano I can borrow?'

'I should think he'll have several. He'll also help you find a place to stay.'

Vinnie glanced at the envelope and read the initials 'LRAM' after the man's name. 'Is this a railway?'

'Vinnie, you can be such a dunderhead. It's the London Royal Academy of Music.'

✳   ✳   ✳

Dobbs knew his own D-Day was coming – Departure Day.

He and Mrs Hall were having tea in the kitchen of the post office. 'There's to be a special train for all you vaccies,' Mrs Hall said. 'And oh, the place won't be the same without you, Dobbs. Watching your gawky legs pushing that bike around the village, like a daddy longlegs on wheels.'

'You'll need to get a stepladder. When I'm gone. I'll come back in five years and find the same stuff on those top shelves.'

'And you'll write, won't you? Tell me how you get on in London. Because I want to know.'

'I will write. Not every day, mind, but I'll write. And it'll be hard when we get to the station. There's going to be tears, Mrs Hall. Crying and blubbing till the train pulls out.'

'Then make sure you've got a very big hanky, you great soft lump.'

* * *

At tea in the vicarage dining room, Kathleen broke the silence. 'The flags are lovely.'

'It's happy and sad,' Mrs Aintree said. 'The thought of what they mean to different people in the village.'

The Reverend Aintree added, 'You'll be another loss to us, Kathleen and Joey.'

'We'll visit,' Joey offered.

'And we may come to London,' Mrs Aintree suggested.

The Reverend Aintree asked, 'How long has it been since you were with your mother?'

Joey said, 'Too long.'

Their mother had had war work, so she hadn't been able to get away to visit them in Netterfold, not even once. It was sort of secret, what she was doing. She couldn't tell them; still couldn't. Not for fifty years.

'Some of the evacuees who came here,' Kathleen said, 'have lost both parents. Father overseas, mother in the bombing.'

'I hope they'll go back to relatives, at least.' Mrs Aintree sighed, then sat nodding.

'And aren't we a cheerful lot?' The Reverend Aintree seemed to rally. 'The war's over and we have a whole world to rebuild.'

* * *

At Netterfold Railway Station, there was only one carriage and a small tank engine to haul it to the main line where it would join the London train. The evacuees said their last farewells to the people who'd looked after them. The elderly porter went along the length of the carriage, ushering passengers into compartments.

Dobbs sang the first line of 'Now Is the Hour', then ushered Kathleen in. He followed and put her bag in the luggage rack. Joey came aboard and swung his case up too, then flopped into a window seat facing the engine.

Vinnie took a last look around the station and waved to Mrs Greenwood. He'd already said good-bye to Miss Armstrong. Her letter was folded in his pocket.

The guard waved a green flag and blew his whistle. The locomotive chuffed and spun its wheels angrily, then got hold of the carriage and eased it out of the station.

Joey said, 'We've been here before.'

'Centuries ago,' Kathleen agreed. 'All we need is Ralph and his chum; then the gang's all here.'

'What was the chum's name?' Vinnie asked. 'I never found out.'

'Algernon or Cedric,' Joey guessed. 'Marmaduke.'

Dobbs asked, 'Vinnie, do you still have your mouth organ?'

'Harmonica.'

'So give us a tune then, maestro.'

Vinnie took out his harmonica, knocked the dust out of it, then began to play 'Beautiful Dreamer'.

Afterword
ANOTHER BOY'S WAR

At some time in mid-September 1939 I became an evacuee, like the children in this story. While Vinnie, Kathleen, Joey and Dobbs are fictional characters, for thousands of boys and girls it was very real. My family lived in Glasgow, which at the time was a large industrial city with factories everywhere and shipbuilding taking place along the River Clyde. The Clyde is where those famous ships the *Queen Mary* and *Queen Elizabeth* were built. So with all that industry, Glasgow and other nearby

LEFT: *The writer, middle row, fourth from left, in a class photograph taken at some time in 1944 or '45. The windows in the back-ground have crisscrossed paper tape on them, while on the extreme right a brick baffle wall can be seen. Both of these were intended as protection against bomb blasts.*

towns and cities were expected to become prime targets for German bombs.

My father had been a soldier in the First War, so he knew what high explosives could do to people and buildings. My family became private evacuees, meaning that my parents arranged it. So we moved with our crockery, pots and pans, blankets and clothes to a smaller town about fifty-six kilometres to the south of the city, on the coast. Those children whose parents couldn't organise a safe billet became public evacuees and often had no idea where they were going or who'd look after them. Evacuees were given luggage labels with their names on them, which they tied on to their clothes with string.

Evacuations took place all over Britain, with children moving from large cities to small rural towns and villages. For many young people who were used to city life, it was a whole new experience to live in the country. Sometimes entire schools were uprooted, so that students travelled with their teachers and settled in different classrooms and dormitories, then picked up their studies where they'd left off. A wartime feature of school life was the criss-crossed paper tape that was stuck over glass windows. This was to prevent the windows being blown in if a bomb fell nearby. For this same reason, my school had tall brick 'baffle' walls built in front of ground-floor windows.

After that first 1939 evacuation, things were quiet for a while. They called this time 'the phoney war', meaning that it wasn't like a war at all. The Germans weren't coming, or so it seemed. Many parents began bringing their children home again, but then in early September 1940 there came the first of many air raids. This was the start of the Blitz, as people called it. 'Blitz' is a German word meaning 'lightning' and comes from the term *Blitzkrieg*, or 'lightning war' – a very fast war. So the period of heavy German bombing over British towns and cities became known as the Blitz.

During the war, there was always the fear of a gas attack, so everyone in Britain was issued with a gas mask, which they had to take with them everywhere. The government supplied the gas mask in a cardboard box with a string for carrying it over your shoulder. It was usual to see a long queue of people waiting to get into the cinema with every single person carrying a gas mask in its box. There were special gas masks for smaller children, such as one that made the child look like Mickey Mouse. For babies, the gas mask was a large affair where the infant was sealed up inside it.

To prevent German bombers finding out which town they were flying over, a blackout was in force everywhere in Britain. It was an offence to show a light from any building at night-time. People had to buy dark cloth curtains or black paper screens for their windows to stop stray light spilling out. Buses and trains also had their windows covered, and there was no lighting in the streets, shop windows or railway stations. There were many accidents during the blackout, because on dark, moonless nights people couldn't see where they were going. Sometimes when a train came into a railway station, passengers accidentally got out of the carriage on the wrong side, then fell on the other railway tracks.

Cars, buses and trucks, and even ordinary bicycles, were able to use their headlights at night, but each vehicle was fitted with cowls that directed the light beam downwards. Drivers painted a white strip around their mudguards so their vehicle could be more easily seen. One shop sold luminous flowers that glowed in the dark and stopped people bumping into each other as they walked along the pavement.

ARP wardens patrolled the streets at night to check that no lights showed. 'ARP' means Air Raid Precautions and wardens, when they saw a glimmer from a window, used to shout, 'Put out that light!' If a person failed to observe blackout regulations, they could be fined. ARP wardens also directed people to special shelters when there was an air raid.

Some people dug their own air-raid shelter in the back garden. They were known as Anderson Shelters, named after a British politician. These shelters were made of sheets of curved corrugated iron, which formed the walls and roof of the structure. The idea was to dig a large hole in the ground, then stick the corrugated sheets in so that they made an arch to form the roof. The earth and turf that had been dug

PUDDINGS & SWEETS

Children should be encouraged to eat their first course of meat, fish or cheese, etc., potatoes and vegetables or salad before they are allowed the sweet course. Puddings and sweets are only tit-bits for filling up odd corners and must not be regarded as the main part of a meal.

Puddings may be rather a problem these days because fat and sugar are rationed and not much of either is left after we have buttered our bread and sugared our tea. However, with care you will probably be able to spare sufficient of these ingredients to make some of the wartime recipes given in this leaflet. Various flavourings can be added to the " basic " recipes to produce a number of different puddings. All recipes are enough for 4 people.

Steamed and Boiled Puddings
Basic Pudding using Mashed Potato

8 oz. flour
2 level teaspoons baking powder
Pinch of salt
2½ oz. fat
2 oz. sugar
2½ oz. mashed potato
Flavouring (any available flavouring may be used)
Household milk to mix

Mix flour, baking powder and salt. Rub in fat, add sugar, potato, flavouring and sufficient milk to mix. Turn into a greased basin and steam for 1 hour.

out of the ground was used to cover the roof of the shelter, to provide extra thickness. Many people built bunks inside their Anderson Shelter, because they had to spend many long nights there when air raids were on. Because they were built over a hole in the ground, the Anderson shelters often flooded with rainwater. At other times they were cold and damp places – frightening, too, as bombs exploded in the distance, or sometimes nearby.

The government also built street shelters, using reinforced steel for extra strength, but these air-raid shelters were still often destroyed and their occupants killed. Schools used their coal cellars as shelters, and children had to carry out regular drills so that everyone knew what to do in an air raid. In London, some underground railway stations were used even when there wasn't an air raid on, because they were deep underground and considered to be safe. As soon as trains stopped running for the night, people would leave their houses and go down to the station platforms with their bedding and blankets. In the morning, when the first underground trains started running, people packed up again and went home.

All over Britain, there was a particular siren sound that signalled when an air raid was to take place. Usually German bombers could be spotted before they reached a major city, so a warning could be given in time. Later in the war the Germans began using rocket bombs, which were harder to see coming, so they took people by surprise. These were known as flying bombs, but Londoners called them doodlebugs. Later, the Germans began using bigger rocket bombs called the V-1 and V-2. All of these flying bombs simply reached the skies over London, then ran out of fuel and began falling to earth. The last V-2 rocket landed in March 1945, only a few weeks before the war ended.

During an air raid, people longed to hear the 'all clear', which was a different siren sound. Then they could leave the shelters and go back to their real beds, but in many cases, people discovered that their house had been hit by a bomb or that half of the street had been flattened.

Britain imported much of its food from overseas, but because of the war it became increasingly difficult to do this. German submarines, or U-boats, hunted in packs, sinking ships that brought supplies into British harbours. The government began to ration food, to make sure every person had enough to eat. Everyone had a ration book that allowed them to buy limited amounts of sugar, butter, tea, meat and so on. Compared with today, it was a very basic diet. The government established a Ministry of Food to help make the best of what food was available. From time to time, recipes were published in newspapers or broadcast on the radio, and even shown in cinemas between movies. These demonstrated ways of making food rations go further.

A famous wartime recipe was Woolton Pie, named after the minister for food, Lord Woolton:

INGREDIENTS

Take 1 pound (500 grams) each of diced potatoes, cauliflower, turnips and carrots; three or four spring onions; one teaspoonful of vegetable extract; and one teaspoonful of oatmeal.

METHOD

Cook all together for ten minutes with just enough water to cover. Stir occasionally to prevent the mixture from sticking. Allow to cool; put into a pie dish, sprinkle with chopped parsley and cover with a crust of potatoes or wholemeal pastry. Bake in a moderate oven until the pastry is nicely brown, then serve hot with gravy.

In my family, a staple of our diet was dried egg, or powdered egg. This was a yellow powder which could be mixed with water or milk, then fried, scrambled or used in recipes.

Every bit of spare land was made available to people in the form of 'allotments' where they could grow vegetables for themselves. In this way, a lot of men and women began to enjoy healthier food as well as getting regular exercise. A government slogan of the time was 'Dig for victory', urging people to grow their own food.

Clothes and shoes were also rationed, and to buy these you needed clothing coupons. There were stories of women who wanted to get married in a

BAKED PUDDINGS

Chocolate Pin Wheels

Pastry—	Chocolate Mixture—
8 oz. flour	2 oz. margarine
1 oz. margarine	4 level tablespoons sugar
4 oz. cooked mashed potato	2 ,, dessertspoons cocoa
2 level teaspoons baking powder	½ teaspoon vanilla essence
Pinch of salt	
Milk or water to mix	

Make pastry and roll out to an oblong shape. Cream margarine and sugar, add cocoa and vanilla essence. Spread mixture on pastry and roll up as for jam roll. Cut into ½ in. slices. Lay slices flat in a baking tin. Bake in a moderate oven for 20—30 minutes.

Two Sweet Fillings for Tarts

Chocolate Filling

3 saccharine tablets or	3 oz. breadcrumbs
1 tablespoon sugar	4 level teaspoons cocoa
½ teacup of milk	A few drops of vanilla
1 reconstituted dried egg	

Dissolve saccharine or sugar in the milk. Beat the reconstituted egg with the sweetened milk. Pour over the breadcrumbs mixed with the cocoa. Beat well in a pan over the heat for a minute or two. Add vanilla. Cool and pour into prepared pastry lining a deep plate. Cover with a pastry lid and bake in a moderate oven for 30 minutes.

Date Filling

4 oz. dates	4 level teaspoons custard powder
4 tablespoons water	1 teaspoon lemon essence

Wash and stone the dates and stew in the water until soft. Add the blended custard powder and lemon essence. Bring to the boil and cook for 2—3 minutes stirring the whole time. Press the dates on the side of the pan to help break them down. Line a tin with pastry and spread over the filling. Bake for 20—30 minutes.

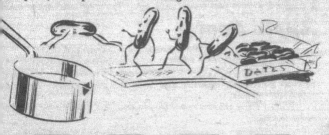

MINISTRY OF FOOD WAR COOKERY LEAFLET 13

bridal gown but didn't have enough coupons to buy the material. Often family members, friends and neighbours would give up their clothing coupons so that the wedding could be as traditional as in pre-war days.

Petrol was also rationed and private motoring was banned, so there were no joy-rides or excursions by car. Sweets and lollies were also in short supply; to buy them you needed what were called 'personal points'. Personal points were included in the ration book. Since rationing developed as the war went on, the books often included coupons or points that were not to be used until people were told. Then when sweets, bread or potatoes had to be rationed, the government announced that those unused coupons could now be used.

Schools went on more or less as they had done before the war, except most of the younger teachers had been enlisted into the armed forces. To fill the gap, many old teachers were brought back out of retirement. Sad to say, a few of them just wanted a quiet life in the classroom, so they taught badly and punished severely.

Pupils often had lectures and warnings about finding and touching what were known as butterfly bombs – small anti-personnel bombs that were packed into a large canister. When the canister was dropped from a German aircraft, it opened and the butterfly bombs fell out. Each one had 'wings' that allowed the bomb to float down and land unexploded. Once on the ground, the butterfly bomb could explode if anyone touched it.

Towards the end of the war, German prisoners came to our school to demolish the baffle walls that had been built to protect us from bomb blasts. Our headmaster warned us very sternly that there was to be no fraternising with the enemy. But the German prisoners were amiable enough and worked cheerfully. They didn't seem to want to be at war any more than we did.

The war intruded into every aspect of life. Our childhood comics, such as *Dandy* and *Beano*, featured funny stories about Addie and Hermie, meaning the German leaders, Adolf Hitler and Herman Goering. In our comics, both were portrayed as greedy and bumbling idiots who could never get anything right. In this way we learned to laugh at our enemies and cheer ourselves up. The New Zealand-born cartoonist David Low worked in Britain for the *Evening Standard* newspaper and was fearless in his cartoon depictions of Hitler and the Nazis. (See page 74 for an example of his artwork.) Hitler in particular was unusually sensitive about such criticism. After the war, it was revealed that David Low had been on the Nazi death list.

Government propaganda was everywhere: on posters and in newspaper advertisements; in cinemas and on the radio. One common message was: 'Careless talk costs lives', meaning that people should be careful of what they said to each other in case they could be overheard. There was a fear that German spies were in Britain, always keen to learn what was going on so they could inform their masters in Germany. Other slogans were: 'Is your journey really necessary?' and 'Coughs and sneezes spread diseases'. And as always, there was the suggestion that people should 'Make do and mend'.

The government propaganda unit also invented 'the Squander Bug' to try to get people to stop spending money on things they didn't need. This was a pretend character shown in newspaper ads and so on, being wasteful. The government preferred people to buy saving certificates or saving stamps. You bought stamps of whatever denomination and stuck them into a book. Later you could redeem the value, plus a small bit of interest.

Another famous wartime slogan was 'V for victory'. Every girl and boy in Britain knew that the morse code for 'V' was *dot*, *dot*, *dot*, *dash*, as in: ••• —. This motif is also heard in the opening of Beethoven's 'Fifth Symphony', which the BBC broadcast to occupied Europe as a sign of hope. Winston Churchill, the British wartime prime minister, often gave the 'V' sign with his fingers.

Since the war played such an important part in people's lives, it wasn't long before it featured in popular songs. Some of these were: 'Who Do You Think You're Kidding, Mister Hitler?', 'There'll Be Bluebirds over the White Cliffs of Dover' and 'We're Gonna Hang Out Our Washing on the Siegfried Line'.

From time to time, there would be flag days: these were ways of raising money from the public. On one of those days, for a penny you could buy a small paper flag to celebrate the Royal Navy, the Army, or the Royal Air Force. There were also public displays designed to cheer people up and show different branches of the armed forces at work. They would exhibit things like a captured German mine or a German bomber that had been shot down.

Most children knew all about German warplanes and what they looked like. Some could even tell an aircraft from the sound its engines made. The names Heinkel, Dornier, Messerschmit and Focke Wulf were well known. We also knew about our own aircraft, especially the Spitfire and the Hurricane fighters. Our bombers were the Stirling, Halifax, Blenheim and Lancaster, and later when the Americans came into the war there were Flying Fortresses.

With so many men and women away fighting in the war, there was a shortage of workers at home. To fill this gap, many women took up work in factories, driving trucks and ambulances, or loading and unloading ships. There was a Women's Land Army, whose job it was to work on the land, at farms, helping to maintain food production. Certain jobs were declared to be 'reserved occupations' though, meaning they were so important to the war effort that the men and women who filled those positions were exempt from military service. Such jobs were coal miners, steel workers, skilled tradesmen in factories and railway-engine drivers.

As well as doing these jobs, many men in reserved occupations did voluntary work at night. Some became ARP wardens, or fire-watchers who stayed up at night in high vantage points to keep a lookout for fires that had been started by German incendiary bombs. Many men joined the Home Guard, a volunteer army whose job it was to guard German prisoners and to defend their local area against attack.

Women, too, did volunteer work, such as with the WVS – the Women's Voluntary Service. They assisted people who had been bombed out of their houses and looked after evacuee children amidst their other duties.

Children at school also did their bit. In my school, they held a competition to see who could collect the most books and magazines. These were sent to the armed services so they could have something to read when they weren't actually fighting. As a prize for the biggest hauls, the lucky boys or girls received a cardboard badge with a rank on it: captain, sergeant and so on. I only received a private's badge, and when the boy who got a captain's badge tried to order me around, we got into a fight.

Despite the war, people still wanted to be entertained, so the cinema became very important. It took the audience's mind off the bad news. The big hit of 1939–40 was *Gone with the Wind*, which people queued for hours to see, and sometimes saw again and again. Boys and girls could attend a Saturday matinee and watch an exciting American adventure film and maybe a Mickey Mouse or Donald Duck cartoon as well as a serial. At home the radio was popular, although in those days it was called the wireless. As the war went on, more and more comedy shows began to appear. For boys and girls there was *Children's Hour* each afternoon.

Sometimes there was an air raid when a film was showing. Since the audience couldn't hear the siren, the projectionist flashed a message on the screen; then everyone went to the nearest shelter.

The day the war ended in Europe – known as 'VE Day' for 'Victory in Europe' – there were celebrations all over Britain, and for the first time, people didn't bother about the blackout. Street-lights came on again. Three months later, the war against Japan also came to an end, giving people an opportunity to celebrate once more.

After it was all over, people in Britain tried to get their lives back together, but it was difficult as so many men and women had died or been seriously injured. Many things had changed. Children, too, had gone through hard times, what with evacuation, fear of air raids, and all the other disruptions to their everyday lives. King George VI recognised this and sent a certificate to every young person in Britain, together with a shilling. The message read:

Today, as we celebrate victory, I send this
personal message to you and all other boys
and girls at school. For you have shared in the
hardships and dangers of a total war and you
have shared no less in the triumph of the Allied
Nations.

I know you will always feel proud to belong
to a country which was capable of such supreme
effort; proud, too, of parents and elder brothers
and sisters who by their courage, endurance
and enterprise brought victory. May these
qualities be yours as you grow up and join in the
common effort to establish among nations of
the world unity and peace.

GEORGE RI

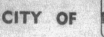

CITY OF LINCOLN

AIR RAID PRECAUTIONS

BABIES ANTI-GAS HELMETS

I have been advised by the Medical Officer of Health of the recent birth of your child.

Arrangements have been made for a Baby's Anti-Gas Helmet to be available for you at the Wardens' Post situated at ....

St. Giles Senior School, Macauley Drive

I am enclosing a record card, and shall be glad if either yourself or some responsible person (preferably your husand) will complete the record card and take it to the Wardens' Post at an early date, when the Helmet will be demonstrated and issued in exchange for the card.

The Helmet remains the property of the Government and will be withdrawn when the child attains the age of two.

If you are changing your present residence permanently to an address **outside the city** the Helmet may be taken with you if prior notification of the address to which you are going is sent to the A.R.P. Officer, 8, Silver Street, Lincoln.

Change of address **within the city** must also be notified.

J. H. SMITH,
Town Clerk.

Acknowledgements

My grateful thanks to Erica Wagner, Publisher of Books for Children and Teenagers at Allen & Unwin, for her unfailing enthusiasm and support in the early stages of preparing the manuscript, and for her wise counsel over these last twenty years or so.

Thanks also to Catherine McCredie, Senior Editor, Penguin Books, who read a very youthful version of the story and made valuable comments.

Editing is that part of a book's production where the author discovers the words and phrases that should have been written in the first place. My gratitude goes to Rosalind Price and Elise Jones, who negotiated the editing with grace, wit and the greatest amiability.

Lastly, to the many girls and boys, and their parents, who lived through those war years: may it never happen again – but then, evacuations still take place all over the world, and in so many different ways.

ABOUT THE AUTHOR

David McRobbie is the author of many bestselling books for children and young adults. He has published more than thirty titles since 1990, and many of his stories have been adapted for television, including the very funny *Wayne* series, *Eugénie Sandler PI*, *Fergus McPhail* and the gripping thriller *See How They Run*. His young adult novel *Tyro* was shortlisted for the 2000 Children's Book Council of Australia Book of the Year Award for Older Readers.

David's background is a varied one: he has worked as a ship's engineer, a primary school teacher, a college lecturer, a parliamentary researcher in Papua New Guinea, and a radio and television producer with the Australian Broadcasting Corporation. He lives in Toowong, Queensland and writes full-time.